Theaker's Quarterly Fiction #56

Edited by
Stephen Theaker
& John Greenwood

Theaker's Quarterly Fiction #56

Edited by
Stephen Theaker
& John Greenwood

Cover Artist

Howard Watts

Contributors

Cam Rhys Lay
Charles Wilkinson
Chuck Von Nordheim
David Penn
Douglas J. Ogurek
Howard Watts
Jacob Edwards
Rafe McGregor

Contents

Films

Editorial

Howard Phillips

To the Rescue

My goodness, how long has it been since I was last asked to write an editorial for this publication? Issue ten, was it? You would think, given that the entire magazine's "success", such as it is, has been founded upon my contributions, that I would be writing editorials for them every other issue. But no, Theaker thinks it's more important for you to see a laughably shallow statistical analysis of his year's reading than to hear from me, his most reliable contributor.

So what has changed this time? Well, sorry to say, Mr Theaker is in no fit state to write an editorial, or anything else. Upon my visit to the TQF offices to deliver my latest manuscript, I found him crying into his moleskine, a shadow of the man who had been such a rock during the more challenging episodes in my life.

As he wept, I could not help but notice the flaccid skin, the untrimmed beard, the scratched glasses, all signifers of a man who had given up on his dignity.

"What's up, Stephen?" I asked, hoping he would not answer.

He wiped away some of the tears before replying. "It has been a difficult couple of months, Howard."

"Oh, I'm sorry to hear that," I said with as much sincerity as I could bring to bear. Which was not a great deal, I have to admit. We all have colleagues like that, do we not, people you might rely on, but whom it would not greatly vex you to see taken down a peg or two. "What has happened?"

"It's stupid," he replied, and I was perfectly willing to believe him. "Four years ago, I noticed that all the reviews on a book seemed to be by the author's friends. All the Amazon reviews, I mean. Except for one, which was less complimentary, and the author's friends were having a go at the reviewer."

"I think I can guess what happened next," I said. "You commented yourself, and pointed out that all the other reviews appeared to be by the author's friends and so you would be more inclined to trust the one that wasn't."

"Yes, how did you guess?"

"We've known each other a long time, Stephen. What happened next?"

He seemed to be pulling himself together. Perhaps it was doing him good to talk about it.

"Not a lot," he said. "A couple of the author's friends commented on the review again to have a go at me, but that made my point for me, so I was happy to leave it there."

"So why are you in tears about it? Four years later?" I was going to need a stiff drink if this went on any longer. But of course Theaker barely drinks a bottle of beer a month, so there was no chance of finding anything with a backbone in his office.

"The author decided to confront me about it on Facebook," Theaker said through his sniffles.

"And of course you apologised for having spoken out of turn, but explained that you felt it your duty to stand up for a fellow reviewer who was coming under fire?"

He shrugged and looked sheepish. "Sort of."

Which is to say, he wrote "Memba this?" and posted

a screenshot of the author using a pseudonym to recommend her own books in the third person. I asked him whether that had helped the situation.

"Not so much," he admitted. "But I showed some restraint. I had half a dozen more screenshots of her doing the same thing, all of them excruciatingly embarrassing, and I didn't post any of those."

I told him to think of someone he admired, and to ask himself whether they would have done the same thing.

"No, they wouldn't, but you would have," he said.

I had to admit that he was right. I would have posted every screenshot all at once, but that is why I do not engage with other authors on Facebook. We are bad for each other.

"Was that the end of it, Stephen? I cannot imagine that such an online altercation would have left you in this state."

He shook his head. "That was only the beginning. She then started a Facebook thread of her own about me. It was clear that all this time she had convinced herself that this incident on the Amazon review was something that I would be embarrassed about, and was surprised to find I didn't mind her bringing it up at all. Now she rallied her friends around, to convince herself that she was in the right, and they said such things about me, Howard, such awful things!"

I asked him for examples, and he opened up the pdf he had created of the conversation in question. Not for him to let Facebook ephemera fade into the dust like so many useless words, no, he had to keep it, cling to his resentments, restoke his righteous anger.

I fear I am beginning to influence the poor boy!

"I don't know where to start," he began. "They said I was 'insignificant', 'unintelligent' (*sic*), a 'troll [who] goes looking for new victims to abuse', 'an arsehole and a t--t', and so on."

"That's terrible!" I said, trying to stifle my laughter. "Do go on."

"One of them said, 'send him this way... I'll even supply the duct tape.'" Theaker shook his head, the tears flying from his face like water from a soggy dog. "The original author called me 'someone with a problem with female genre writers.'" (I tactfully didn't bring up how few female genre writers had appeared in his zine of late.) "She then said my 'accusations are persistant (*sic*) and focused ... almost like stalking.'"

It was almost adorable how he would mispronounce the words that had been spelt incorrectly and then say *sic* afterwards, as if the bad spelling in some way negated the criticism.

"Was that the worst of it?" I asked, crossing my fingers that there would be more.

"No, it wasn't," he said, looking me in the eyes with the utmost seriousness. "One of them said, 'I just hope someone posts a photo of his needle dick so we can all laugh at him.'"

I could not prevent myself from laughing out loud this time, to his great dismay. I patted him on the shoulder. "It's not you I'm laughing at, dear fellow. What a peculiar thing to hope for! But surely that is no longer upsetting you? It's funny rather than anything else, a bunch of wallies making themselves look foolish."

He shrugged. "I did notice one thing, that despite people in the thread asking to be given my name so that they could block me as a troll, none ever did, presumably because giving those people my name would have led them to my side of the story."

"That's the spirit, lad!"

"And the author did admit that the reviews on Amazon *were* all by her friends, and she confirmed that the sockpuppet on Amazon *was* indeed her."

"There you go," I thundered. "A good day's work! So

why didn't you put all of this on Twitter, drum up a social media storm, take her down once and for all?"

He shook his head. "Times have changed, Howard. Haven't you read Jon Ronson's book, *So You've Been Publicly Shamed*?" (I haven't, of course. I rarely read books I didn't write myself.) "What does it really matter if one silly author is saying silly things about me, especially when she's not mentioning me by name? Bringing the internet crashing down on her head would be disproportionate."

"You're just getting soft," I said, kicking him in the shins. "Why are you still crying about it?"

"That was just the start of a bad couple of months," he replied. He went on to tell me an epic tale of power and paranoia, but if you think I'm going to tell you that story, forget it. Find your own plot for your next novel. That one's mine!

In This Issue

We have six stories for you in this issue, some of them practically novellas. They are arranged roughly in chronological order, so if you like fantasy start at the beginning, and if you like science fiction start at the end! We also have over sixty pages of reviews!

Contributor News

If you have ever contributed to this zine, you'll probably know that we have a long-standing offer to run free advertisements for suitable projects in the magazine. And if you don't, it's because Stephen forgot to say, but it still applies! It's a way of making him feel better about exploiting you all.

We thought it might be nice to collect smaller bits of news from contributors too, for a section in the

magazine, for our new email newsletter, maybe also
for blog posts, if there were enough to make a blog
post worthwhile.

So if you've been a contributor to the magazine, and
have any news about what you're up to now, or are
likely to have any news in future, here's the link.
Bookmark it and let us know whenever you've got
something going on:

https://docs.google.com/forms/d/1iwBL6hKiI7svNo
Wi8IlouFRiuH4Rrw16X8cESsfTafo/viewform

For example:

Rafe McGregor's seventh book, *The Value of
Literature*, was due for publication by Rowman &
Littlefield International in hardback in August 2016
and in paperback in February 2018.

Douglas J. Ogurek's unsplatterpunk extravaganza
"Maim Street" was selected for *The Best Weird Fiction
Vol. 6* (Morpheus Tales Publishing). *Prick of the
Spindle* published his satirical piece "Thomas
Sageslush's Support of the Moronvia Heights Pit Bull
Ban". *The Literary Hatchet* (PearTree Press) picked up
his oft-anthologized (and highly juvenile) "Stool Fool".
And *The Great Tome of Forgotten Relics and Artifacts*
(Bards and Sages Publishing) featured his "The
Binding Agent".

---

*Howard Phillips feels obliged to help out when
Stephen is feeling low, even though he knows this is not
the original Stephen he knew, merely the Stephen of
this new bubble universe. Howard is working on a new
novel.*

Concerning Strange Events at the Manor of Sir Hugh de Villiers, Valiant Knight

From MS. Janaway D. vii (about 1380), transcribed from the Middle English by David Penn

I, Geoffrey of Melverley, of the Abbey of Angelsbury in the county of Shropshire, do make a record of these things that I may believe them myself, and peruse them in after days and consider: Yes, that happened, and that happened, and I was that poor fool, flung into a vipers' pit of strange and sorrowful destiny. For these things that I witnessed and took part in are so fantastical that if I only open my eyes upon daylight, they seem a dream, even a blasphemous one.

And certainly while I live, I may tell no man of these events, for all would think me mad, or else would doubt my steadfastness in the Church, or worse; and there are reasons greater than that also for my silence. But I will leave my secret pages for others that come after me, since they may understand better than I do myself the things I try here to record. Therefore have pity on me any that read, for it is a woeful tale, and I hate my own part in it. I know not whether I did right or wrong, but if I did make error, may the Lord in His mercy forgive me, for I acted in good will.

It began thus. In the year of our Lord thirteen hundred and sixty-four, the thirty-eighth year of the reign of our Sovereign Edward III, in October, a messenger came to our lovely abbey in great haste, and asked for me. It was a cold, damp morning and he had travelled far, so while his horse was watered and fed we took him to the warming room. There, he stood heaving from his ride until he was able to tell me that my cousin, Sir Hugh de Villiers, a great Knight of Shropshire, had asked for me and wished urgently to see me.

Now my Lord Sir Hugh de Villiers was a man of renown and worship in these parts, and though he was my cousin, my grandfather's brother's son, I had heard no word from him for many a year. So I wondered at this request. By God's grace I am a warden in this fair brotherhood of ours, but that is only to be one of many, and I am no great man, either in the Church or among my own people, to come to the mind of such a knight. Also, though my Lord de Villiers' manor lies to the south-west, and that is the quarter that falls under my office, his lands are his own, not the abbey's, and I had no cause to visit them. Why then should this great knight send his man to call upon me?

The messenger, who was called Guillaume, would give no reason, but said that my cousin was soon to go to Christ, and lay in his last bed, and we must not dally here and waste time. These last words seemed unmannerly to me, but I saw that this servant loved his master dearly, so I did not rebuke him. Also I began to fear, from his distress, that my cousin should require absolution for some grievous sin, and had asked for me especially because of our kinship. So I called for a horse and a pack to be made ready for my journey, and went with this Guillaume to see his master.

The journey was long, for my kinsman's lands lay at Woodmoor, through much marshy country. Nevertheless, after we had stayed a night at a church house in Worthen, we arrived, by the Grace of God, before the next evening had set in.

Now my good cousin Sir Hugh de Villiers had a great castle, and from its battlements he might survey many and many an acre, and all the land he saw was his. It was before this eagle's eyrie now that I sat upon my horse marvelling at its powerful walls, and in truth trembling a little, while my Lord's men lowered the drawbridge over the moat. For my kinsman was a famous man of war, long favourite of our gracious King Edward, and men told many tales of his deeds at Crécy and Calais. They said he had brought back many strange things, even animals, for his own amusement, from his travels after those battles, and the countries that he had passed through. And as I looked upon the castle I could not help but think on these stories and ask myself again in wonder: What should this mighty man of valour and captain of men want of me? But this thought sustained me: that God may will it, and it is God that the man truly wants, not my poor self.

As we rode across the drawbridge, my kinsman's men looked down upon me, some with a mean eye, and one joked to the messenger: "Hye, Guillaume, who is this monk on a horse? Another of our Lord's bastards?" There was much merriment, and I saw that Guillaume too laughed a little, until I turned my eye upon him in meek rebuke; but I held my tongue, for the Lord is my Shepherd among these wolves. Yet I thought in my heart as we crossed and as I looked about me at the moor, barren of anything but red bracken and pale crags: Yes, here is an evil place, that breeds sickness and a wicked brood, for this is a vile and wasted land. Even the Lord, when he wreaked his vengeance upon our sinful country with the Pestilence, spared it nothing. I think it is because there are pagans and witches here, though my Father Abbot chastises me for my uncharity. But do we not know that we live in evil times?

In the courtyard Guillaume bade me leave my horse and follow him into the castle. Inside all was quiet and dark, except that here and there a few servants bustled, fewer than I have seen in any great house, even the most desolate ones that I visit on my rounds. There was a fire in the hall but no one by it. Guillaume took me by a narrow staircase, which taxed me severely, to an upper chamber, where lay my Lord Sir Hugh upon his bed, a small fat man with a bald pate, though with thick strong arms. He was sore afflicted, his skin yellowish, and by his side sat a young man dabbing at his face with a cloth. As I entered, this youth stopped his work and watched me with eyes that were as black as his long thin locks.

Guillaume swept his arm wide toward me to show his master that he had accomplished his task by bringing me for this counsel, and Sir Hugh thanked his servant in very kind and affectionate terms, and charged him to fetch me wine and something from his kitchens to eat.

"Please sit, Father, my good cousin," said my Lord, and pointed to a couch on the other side of his bed from the boy who attended him. "And please forgive the insolence of my son, Otto." Even at this rebuke, the boy at first did no more than dip his head at me, until his father admonished him further to stand and greet me in a proper manner; then, with ugly grimaces, he rose and bowed. He had a brazen look, certainly, albeit that he was not yet eighteen years of age, as I guessed.

"I thank you that you have come. I am sorry that I cannot let you rest, but God willing, the repast that Guillaume brings you will atone for that ungraciousness. In truth, I have little time and I must do some business with you before I depart this world. I have heard well of you through the mouths of some who know you in this county, and they tell me that you prosper in your calling, and not long ago were ordained a priest."

I told him that this was so, and that my Father Abbot had encouraged me, because, he said, a warden monk should also be a priest, the better to attend the needs of his flock on his rounds, as he collects rents from the bailiffs and agrees repairs. As I spoke, I saw that again the man's son looked at me with hatred. I thought that perhaps he did not like holy men, as many do not in these times, and that he deemed his father weak and foolish in his illness for confessing. But I forgave him in my heart and leant toward my Lord to hear of his sin and desire for absolution. Yet he made no such request.

"Father, my Cousin Geoffrey," said Sir Hugh. "It will be a long night for you. I have brought you here to charge you with a grave duty as a kinsman and man of our Holy Church. I will have need of all your talents and kindness before this night is out. But first you must hear something from me: you must hear my strange tale, perhaps the strangest you have yet heard, or are likely to hear."

I sat back, with some impatience in my heart I confess, but nodded to show I would listen to whatever my cousin wished to tell me. Truly the tale was as strange as my Lord had warned.

"You know that I fought with Edward's noble armies in France," Sir Hugh began, "where thank God, at that time, we were victorious. That was eighteen years ago, and since then weaker men have not served the King so well I think, but perhaps that is not for me to say. After our great battles at Crécy and other places, I grew sick of warfare and requested permission to go on pilgrimage. Our gracious Sovereign gave me leave, and I went to the Holy Land, with only my good attendant Guillaume and no other, because in two years of fighting I had seen too many men, and I yearned for my own company and the peace of far roads.

"I passed through a score of countries and everywhere saw things I had never before imagined, and had many adventures. Yet the strangest adventure I ever had was in my own country, in England, in the Forest of Arden in Warwickshire, so near to this my own home.

"When I came back to England, it was with a heavy heart. For I had seen the devastation in all Europe wrought by the Pestilence, and I was sorely afraid of what I would find here. Certainly, there was as much death and affliction and misery as there was in any other country. For me, in my own person, Fortune was favourable perhaps, because the main terror of that great sickness had passed when I came back to our shores. Yet heavy tidings indeed awaited me, for when I came to London and saw my friends and kinsmen in that city, they told me that Philippa my beautiful wife had died, and so too my eldest son. I grieved for them as I rode, for I wasted no time in coming back to my own lands, though in truth I said in my heart: 'Why do I ride so fast? There is nothing for me at home.'

"It happened that in Warwickshire, as I was passing with Guillaume through a village where we hoped to gain bed and board for the night, I saw that the folk there were badly oppressed, and poor, with little to eat and only rags to wear. Nowhere on my travels had I seen such a miserable place as this. So poor were they, they could hardly find us food for a small repast, though I showed them coin.

"I asked: 'What is wrong here? It is as though the Devil himself marched in the valley.'

"They said: 'Yes, Sir Knight, you speak truly, for if it is not the Devil that blasts 978-1-910387-17-7ur fields and our cattle and our houses, it is his servant, for this place in one year has become Hell. We had the Pestilence here very badly, but this is worse, and we do not know what we have done to offend God that this should befall us.'

"So I asked 'What is this fiend?'

"Another replied: 'It takes the guise of a giant, but it is covered with the scales of Hell.'

"I was amazed, for has not God with the aid of his saints and knights rid this land of giants and monsters that once assailed humanity? Men love to tell of many fabulous beasts, but only the oldest and most barbarous tales speak of such things in England. I turned to Guillaume and he shook his head with a questioning look.

"'Yes, Sir Knight,' said another; 'God gave us warning enough, but the wicked of this village, and our Lord away in the manor, did not listen. The Lord God sent His sign, a falling star, and then this fiend came.'

"All the village folk nodded that were around our horses, and a man called Perkin, who among them seemed a kind of leader, said: 'Stay awhile and you shall see him for yourself. For he has no fear of man.'

"Perkin and his son took us to the fields where a neighbour was labouring. The corn lay flat and blasted, and in another field were piled the carcases of cows, flesh ripped from their bones and their throats rent and gaping. Trembling as he spoke, Perkin told me this had happened in the night, when these abominations were always done.

I said, because I was unable to believe: 'And this is not the work of men?'

"Perkin said: 'No, this work, all of it, was done in a moment. No man could do such a thing and none was seen – only a screaming fiend, for my neighbour saw these things with his own eyes. And he is a good Christian who drinks little and is no liar. It is the work of Satan.'

"I looked upon this butchery and at these people with pity, and the neighbour came and we burned the cows and saved what we could of the crop.

"Now they had sent to their Lord in his manor for help, but none had come. They said Sir Guy, for that was this Lord's name, had heard stories of the creature, and some of his servants had seen it and its works and fled, even to tell him. But he would give no assistance; only, he said, he would reduce the tithe for a season, but the villagers said that helped no one.

"So I told them that I would do what I could to aid them, because I am bound by knightly oath to protect good Christians, and all the poor and lowly such as they. Truly also, if I lost my life now, what of it? For without my wife and firstborn, I have none. So I said in my heart.

"And I told them: 'Very well, I shall wait here in this field tonight until I see the creature. Tether a cow in the middle of the field and I shall watch what this thing will do.' And the man Perkin and his neighbour spoke together and agreed to my request.

"So at sundown a cow was dragged to a post. Guillaume served me bread and water that the villagers had given us, and I sat behind a tree, and they bade us goodnight and thanked me and ran home. I told Guillaume to go with them, though at first he would not. Then I settled against the trunk. It was a cold night, as this is, and I would sleep, but I knew that such thoughts were temptations of Satan and I kept awake with my sword in my hand.

"When it was not yet midnight I saw that the trees in the wood, on the other side of the field, began to move, and at the same time I heard a growling as of a dog. I confess that I grew very afraid, for I had fought many an enemy in my life but never one such as this; and noble or low-born, good or bad, they had always been human enemies.

"Now the trees broke apart and a creature as from a dream came out into the field. And in all the world's tales of dragons and monsters, cyclopes, chimeras, gorgons and other such things, and all pictures of such beasts that men like to draw, nothing was ever like this. It was as tall as two men and walked upright as a man does, and had a mouth like a great gate. Its arms trailed on the ground and it had on each of them ten fingers that ended in claws as long and sharp as daggers.

"When it saw the cow, the creature gave a roar and ran to it and, with one swipe of its talons, slit its throat; then it lifted the cow to its mouth and began to eat. There was a stink like sulphur and I thought: 'That is the stink of Hell' and I felt the fear of death itself, but I had given my oath to the people of the village and I ran from my tree shouting, with my sword in my hand.

"And I was amazed because the beast screamed also and dropped the cow into the mud and opened its arms wide. I saw the favour that God had granted me and thrust my sword into its middle. Black blood flooded onto the blade and my hand, and I pulled my weapon free ready to strike again.

"But the creature fell, howling and holding its belly, and dug the ground with its claws. I raised my sword over its head, but the beast struck out and took it from my hand and threw it far away. I ran to take my sword and made myself ready to strike again but now the monster stood upright on its legs and turned towards the wood. And I asked myself: 'The thing is dying. Where is it going? Surely it must have a home in the woods, and there may be more of its kind in that home.' So, though I feared greatly still, I pledged in my heart that as I had overcome this beast, I would follow it and make sure that there were no others that might blight the village more.

"The creature walked a little and fell and crawled and cried out in great pain, and though I believed it to be a devil of Hell, I began to pity it. For whatever it was, do not all living things suffer the same way? I might have ended its agonies with a blow of my sword but that I thought of the villagers, and the great troubles they might face if I left the beast any fellows or brothers to wreak vengeance upon them.

"So the monster crawled and panted and heaved itself up and walked a little way, and fell again, and I followed, and I saw that not once did it turn on me or offer me any fight. And truly, though this creature had done wrong, I began to sorrow of what I had wrought. For in its actions, as it rested against trees and looked back towards me and again ahead, and fell and tried to stand, I began to question whether this strange beast might not possess intelligence and some understanding, not unlike a man's.

"Then after long effort it came upon a track up to a crag, and as I followed along this track I saw that the creature was struggling towards a cave.

"And the smell of this cave was worse than the stink of war, which I know well, or of filth or ordure. I held my hand to my mouth for fear of vomiting.

"Now also I heard a sound, as of foxes calling at night, and I followed the thing into its cave, and what I saw there made my senses spin. For this was like the Pit itself. I cannot describe it otherwise.

"On the floor was grass and straw, and among this, the rotting flesh and skins of many animals, and their bones, white in the moonlight. But far stranger than this, hanging from the cave's roof were what seemed giant cradles of some substance like that of cobwebs, that dripped with a thick white liquid. In one of them was another creature like the one I had smitten, but utterly still, and dead. Yet more amazing to my eyes, watching uncertainly from the back of the cave were two beasts again in all ways like that now crawling towards them, calling to them, but not one twelfth of its size. And I realised they were its children.

"The little animals gathered around their parent like cubs around a she-wolf, crying and mewling, and their parent vomited forth flesh, and its offspring ate. And I began to question in myself if this creature that I had wounded were male or female, mother or father, because in nature it is the female that oftenest feeds the little ones, and after that in my heart I knew this great beast to be the whelps' mother. And because of her dealings with her cubs and because I saw that their eyes, though hooded and black, were bright, I understood for certain that these, mother and children, were no brutes but thinking creatures, as I am.

"Then the mother died, and her pups set up a great wailing, and I felt ashamed, and fully repented of what I had done.

"I had a duty to the villagers, who had charged me with the destruction of their tormentor, but I knew that I could not kill her cubs. So I cut off her head and tied it to my saddle, and took off my cloak and carried the little creatures in it on my back. I took the monster's head to the villagers to show that I had accomplished my task, and their fields and cattle and homes were safe. And they made a great cheer, but they said 'What is in your cloak?' for they heard noises from it and saw there the shapes wriggling and contorting that I could not conceal, so I said 'That is my booty, my treasure, in payment for the deed I have done you'. They said 'Very well' but drew near as if to touch the sack that I had made from my cloak, until Guillaume came beside me and I glared at them and touched my sword, and they drew back and troubled us no further. I put the bundle over my saddle and we rode that morning for home, for it was near dawn already.

"As we came into Shropshire, and my own lands here, I began to grieve again, more severely, for I thought of my lost wife and firstborn.

"In truth, at the gates of my castle there were few to greet me, for the Pestilence had cut so many from my household, and I held the only son left to me, Otto here, to my bosom, and my daughter Mathilda also, who was living then. For Mathilda too died, some years later, when more fevers came amongst us.

"I showed no one my two young creatures, but shut them in a dungeon, and bade Guillaume build a place of concealment for them, in a wooded part of my land, where there is a cave. With other men of my manor, though they knew not what they did, he built a chamber for my captives, large enough for them even when they grew to their mother's size, with iron bars within the cave, and a secret door, that no eye should see them. For I had said in my heart that I would keep them here on my own land, for the pity I bore them.

"Certainly the men spoke in their villages of the chamber they had helped to build. And because of that and the creatures' roaring and crying at night, many folk in this county say that I have brought lions or wolves from the Holy Land, or from my wars, as bounty, and that I feed poachers to them; but no one, besides Guillaume and Otto, knows what I have there, and as for the tales people tell, let them be told, for if folk are afraid to come prying on my lands, then that is a blessing."

There my Lord rested, and sank back into his cushions, and the lad mopped his brow again.

Now I was astonished at this tale, and I would certainly have disbelieved all of it, except that the man's son Otto had shown no sign of demur throughout its telling. Even so I thought it may have been that the good knight was out of his wits and his son also, or that the son dare not disagree.

But Sir Hugh saw my confusion and laughed and said: "In a little while you will believe, for you shall see with your own eyes."

Now Guillaume came with a small roast fowl and wine, and water in a bowl, and I washed my hands and ate and drank, but when I had finished Sir Hugh bade his son and his servant take me to the place where he said the creatures were confined.

Night had fallen by this time and Otto and Guillaume took torches to light our way, and they led me out of the castle and along a path that went into the forest. Here the path became thick and dark with trees overhanging and I shook as I walked, because I did not know what I should see, and I wondered in my heart at these men, what they truly wanted of me; for, whatever Sir Hugh had said, are there really monsters and giants among us in these days? Otto, seeing my fear, laughed and began to run ahead, and then again behind me, and to shout suddenly and pummel me with small stones and acorns, which I confess filled me with terror in that place. I saw that Guillaume would have him cease but dare not say anything. And I thought if there really were a demon in that forest, then surely it was no one but Otto. But Guillaume was kind and walked beside me.

Now the path began to twist and turn upwards through a steep and craggy place, and we came to a door that had been set in the rock. Guillaume took a key from his pouch and opened it, and immediately I heard a terrible roaring, and there was a stench like pitch and sour eggs and burning wood all together, and I thought: "Perhaps the knight does in truth keep lions here, and I shall be their meal tonight." Again I trembled, and would have turned back, but that I am a man of God, and must show the courage of God, and I thought of Daniel in the lions' den, whom the Lord saved.

Now the stench grew past enduring and the sounds became so loud that I covered my ears, and Otto laughed, but we went to another door and Guillaume took another key and opened it, and we stood at the top of some steps, cut in the rock.

There before me was truly the strangest and most terrible thing that has ever passed my vision. For in the light of our torches I saw a great cage of wood and iron, as tall as two storeys of a house, rising to the roof of the cave; and set in the roof was a small grate. And among straw within this cage sat two creatures, giants now, for in the time since the knight had captured them, they had grown to the size of their parent. And if they were not demons from Hell, I did not know what they were but great imps or goblins that the common people speak of, for as Sir Hugh had said they were like no other creature on God's earth that any man knows. They were black and thick in body, with long arms, and had great mouths that opened and closed continually, showing teeth like rows of spikes, and the black eyes of demons. Big as they were, they sat holding each other in strange manner like children, and watching me. Guillaume led us down the steps to stand before the cage, but there I fell to the ground, and said "Jesus Christ deliver me" and Otto pulled me to my feet and said: "Look, monk, upon God's creation."

I said: "If these are creations of God, they have turned from Him because truly they are devils", but Otto said "No, for do devils eat and shit and sleep as these do?" and he laughed.

I said "I do not know" and he took out his sword and thrust it into their cage, and they shrank back. He said "Are devils afraid of a man's sword?" and I said, "I do not know; but if they are not devils, then what manner of creature are they?"

"They are the sons of the giantess that my father slew, that is all, for he told you the truth. And now we must feed them."

Then Guillaume took from his sack great pieces of beef, and bones, which he had taken from the kitchen, and threw them into the cage, and the creatures darted forward and took the meat and pressed it into their mouths with their great clawed hands, and the stink, like sulphur, again grew worse.

Otto threw a stone at them and they cowered back, mewling piteously, and I saw that Guillaume did not like what the boy did, but again he dared not speak against him.

But now as the creatures sat and ate in silence, Guillaume brought his torch closer to the bars of their cage, and I looked inside and gaped. For in that mighty chamber were two great cots for sleeping and a cask of water, as in a cell for men, even a monk's cell; and heavy drapes hung against the wall at the back; but more strange than this, upon a great table that stood in front of the wall was a book, and behind that a cross, even the Holy Rood of our Lord Jesus Christ.

I turned to Guillaume and said: "Why is the Lord's Cross set there, with these monsters?"

He said: "Father, my Lord Sir Hugh put it there."

I looked again, to know whether my eyes deceived

me, and said: "Is the Cross of Our Saviour meet for such creatures as this? Is it not blasphemy to put it there? For if they are not demons, then still they are no more than animals, and loathsome ones."

But Guillaume said: "My master believes that they are neither demons nor animals, but that they understand speech, and even that they understand scripture, and he often sits in this chamber with them and recites to them from his psalter, that you see there, into which he has copied many parts of the Holy Word himself, and they do not harm him or even make any noise, but listen in peace."

I could not believe what he told me, or even the sights I could myself see, and held my hands to my face in my distress, and wondered above wondering: "What strange trial is this that God has given me?" I said to the servant: "I cannot bear it; please let us go back to your master", and Guillaume led the way out of the cave and Otto again laughed.

And all the way back along the path I was greatly troubled, but gathered myself for the sake of Sir Hugh.

At his bedside I admonished him severely, though I was sick in my stomach. "I do not know what these creatures are that you have shown me, whether some new brood of Satan or mere beasts and monsters, but it is surely sacrilege to give the Holy Rood and a book of Scripture to them, just as it is to cast sacred things among bears and dogs." As I spoke I shook, for the image of the creatures would not leave my mind.

Sir Hugh smiled and closed his eyes and said: "Good Cousin, sit down, and please take some wine, for I know what terror it is to first set eyes on those strange wards of mine."

I drank deeply from the cup that Guillaume brought me; and when I had done so, my Lord began again: "Now, you have seen what you have seen, flesh and blood, and you have the proof of all that I have told

you. But as to your question about my captives, and
the holy things I gave them: You will know better than
I, but if they were demons could they abide the Cross
or to hear the Word of God? Would they not shrink
from it? And if they were animals, would Scripture
sooth them, as I have seen, as it does any flock in a
Church?"

I did not know what to say for I still feared for my
Lord's sanity, if not my own as I trembled, and could
only ask in my heart for God's guidance. But my cousin
had something further to say to me:

"Father Geoffrey, strange as they are, I took these
creatures from their mother, whom I killed; I took pity
on them and brought them here, to my own lands,
where they have dwelt for fourteen years. I have
watched them. I have seen them affectionate with one
another and I have seen them watching and listening
to everything around them, and I believe them to have
intelligence, the same as men. I believe them to be
God's creatures, as we ourselves are, and not Satan's.

"Cousin, I have not much time, and I must ask some
service of you, if you will listen: Will you baptize my
captives into our Holy Mother Church? Also, when I
am dead, will you watch over them? My son Otto will
keep them, but I fear he does not love them as I do.
Neither does he feel my sin as I do, in killing their
mother. Therefore I believe he will not look after them
well. So I beseech you: come here sometimes, on your
rounds, and see that the creatures are well cared for.
And the other thing I ask is that you watch over my
son, that he does not take the path of evil, as I fear. I
have no other relatives living who can perform this
office, so great is the havoc that the Pestilence has
wrought on my family."

I looked at Otto and he glared at me as before, and
now I understood why he did not like me, because his
father wished to put him in my care, at least in part,

and certainly in the matter of his soul. Even so it was not the care of Otto, but my Lord's first request that troubled my heart, and that deeply. I could not speak in my confusion.

"Cousin I beseech you," Sir Hugh said again.

"My Lord, gladly would I visit your son and advise him as I am able, but as for the other: do you know what you ask of me? Whatever these creatures may be, they are not men, with souls. It is surely blasphemy and a sacrilege against a holy rite to baptize them. It is an abomination."

"I have told you what I believe them to be," said the knight, and pulled at his bedclothes, and called Guillaume to come with water for his brow. "And what I say is true, for I have sat with them many a day all these years. Yet, think as you may, tell me: Where in the Scriptures does it say that you may not baptize an animal, or a demon, come to that, if it repents? If it is so, I have not heard it, and I am a Christian man and have heard many teachings in church and out of it, though I am no scholar, I confess."

In truth I have never read in any scripture expressly that we may not baptize an animal, nor yet any manner of creature. But I shook my head and said: "Has any man heard of a demon that repents?" And then: "It is the teaching of Christ and of His Church that baptism is for man, who has an everlasting soul, and not for animals, nor for that matter stones or trees. Or do you say that these beasts of yours are of another creation, of which God has not told us, and they too have everlasting souls? If you answer 'yes' you must tell me where in church or out of it you heard that teaching."

"And if they are intelligent creatures, able to understand Scripture, and if they are like man and have immortal souls, and you do not baptize them, what will the Lord have to say to you, Cousin, on the Day of Judgement?"

I was angry at this impudence and rose and said: "It is not given to us to know what the Lord will say to any man on that day," and Otto laughed and Sir Hugh cursed him. But I thought in my heart: "This is the trial that God has set me." I went to the window that looked down on the courtyard and leant with my hand on the wall beside it, and my hand shook; then I turned and said to the great knight: "I have seen your creatures, as you say, and still I do not know if I may believe my own eyes. But what you tell me now, of their nature, I find yet harder to comprehend. My Lord, can you truly tell me that those things have understanding?"

He said: "I tell you the truth. I have asked them questions concerning the Holy Word and they have shown me by signs that they understand."

I looked at him and, even in my fear, above all I pitied him. I knew that I was there for a purpose, and that must be God's purpose, and I saw that my cousin was a good man, a man of God, and I thought: "The Lord is bounteous in his mercy. His love is without limit. Whatever strange pass He has brought me to, whatever these creatures are, if I baptize them and bring peace to this good knight's heart, then surely God will not punish me, or my kinsman. It may be, even, that to bring these creatures somehow to His grace is God's wish. Perhaps they are not what they seem. Or yet, it may be that though I baptize soulless things, and do them no good, it will increase Sir Hugh's faith, and that of his son and servant, and that is the Lord's plan." Yet in my heart I was not certain, and I asked for some moments to pray.

And my Lord said: "Cousin, I well understand your need. Guillaume will lead you to our chapel here and

you may pray and seek God's guidance as you wish.
But let us hope it is not too long coming."

I bowed and thanked my Lord, and Guillaume took
me down the staircase again and through many
passages to Sir Hugh's small chapel. And I went before
the altar and begged God to direct my steps, according
to His purposes.

It seemed I knelt long, and my mind was full only of
the terrible things I had seen and heard in the cave:
the creatures' great jaws, their dripping teeth as they
tore at the meat they were fed, and Otto's laughing.
And once more I was sick within at these things.

But then at last it seemed to me that my heart
stilled, and a wonderful scent grew strong in the
chapel, the scent of incense. And it came to my mind
how often Sir Hugh and his household must come to
this place and pray and give thanks. And I saw Sir
Hugh praying there with me and all his family, even
the dead, his wife and eldest son, as though full of life.
And the knight's heart glowed like a fire within him,
and God reached down and took it in His hands. And I
threw myself down before the Lord and wept that he
had blessed me with such a vision; then I rose and
crossed myself and left the chapel. For I knew what
these signs meant: that Sir Hugh was a good man,
beloved of God, and I may trust his wishes.

I went back to my cousin and said: "I will do as you
say" and he wept and told me that if I promised to
come to watch over the creatures and his son, if only
once in a season, he would make a great gift to the
abbey, and I would be the cause of it.

And I blessed him.

Now Sir Hugh wished me to act straight away, for he
said again that he was dying. Guillaume brought me a
bowl of water he had taken from the chapel font, and a
little salt from the kitchens, which I also asked for, and

he and Otto took me again to the cave wherein the creatures sat.

Guillaume stood by me at the bars of the cage, holding the bowl for me, and spoke to the beasts, calling them to come near, but they would not come until Otto moved away and went and sat on the steps. Then they came a little way towards me, crossing the floor on their wide front claws as much as their feet, as lizards walk, with strange rolling movements, and all the time they did not take their eyes from me. Their terrible countenance and their stink, especially as they drew closer, filled me again with fear, but I called on the Lord for courage, and my fear grew less as I prayed. But yet I could not begin the sacrament. Guillaume gave me a questioning look, and I heard Otto curse behind me, but for some moments I could do nothing but gaze into the cage.

For again I could not understand why I had been chosen, of all men, to bear witness in this way to such strange things, and be the instrument of God's plan for these creatures or for Sir Hugh, whatever that might be: I, who so lack courage. And I looked into their eyes, which so strangely looked back at me, and their mouths that gaped, as infants gape in the crib, and the scales they bore, and was filled with wonder that here may be creatures that, though they looked like nothing else in all Creation, may have intelligence, if all Sir Hugh believed were true. And I thought: for certain, men do not understand the ways of God, and it is only in our false pride that we believe we are able to. And then my Maker again so filled me with His love, and so sustained me, that I forgot my fear, and I gathered myself to perform the baptism.

I blessed them, and asked them questions of their faith, to which truly I do not know whether their strange gestures and mewlings were answers or not; and though I dared not reach into the cage to touch them, I made the sign of the Cross before each of them. Guillaume gave me the sack of salt he had brought, and I dipped my hand in it and licked the salt from my fingers, letting the creatures see clearly what I was doing, then threw handfuls of it at them through the bars of their cage. They flinched back growling but then lapped the salt from their faces and arms with their long tongues, as I had hoped, for salt is for the cleansing of evil from the body and must enter through the mouth. And now I watched, for I thought: "Truly, this will be a test: for if they are demons after all, surely the salt will burn them." But it did not harm them.

So now I baptized them in the name of the Lord, sprinkling them with water from the bowl that Guillaume held, and prayed for them, and for Sir Hugh and all his household, and for myself. Afterwards the beasts did nothing, but only watched me, and moved back again deeper into their cage, and even now I trembled to think what I had done.

But I went back and told my kinsman that I had fulfilled his wish, and he smiled; and not many days after that, he died, and they say he died in peace.

Now Otto became master of all his father's lands and riches, and soon all that the good knight had feared came to pass, for the whole country was full of tidings of his son's evil deeds, and the people quaked at his very name. For they said he and his friends took women from the villages, and slew any man that quarrelled with them, and that the good knight's castle was no nobleman's home any more but a brothel.

But I remembered my promise to the boy's father, and I went, though in fear, to Woodmoor. At first Otto would not allow me entrance, but I called upon the name of his great parent, and he relented. And although it was yet but midday, he was drunk, and sat at dice with two companions. He rose and cursed me to my face, but I begged him to come outside the chamber with me and asked him in a quiet voice: "Let me see your father's creatures, as I promised."

Then to my sorrow he shouted, so that his companions could hear: "Ah, good monk: you wish to see those monsters that my father kept for our pleasure?" And he took me in to his friends and they laughed, and I understood that Otto had not kept his father's secret, at least from these men.

He said: "You come too late, for they are dead", and grinned, and strode from me saying: "In truth, monk, I do not know whether they are dead or alive. Go and see them; but this once only and no more, for you may never come to my lands again."

And he called Guillaume, and stood with his companions and watched me with hateful eyes, as the servant and I departed.

So Guillaume took me out of the castle and along the path once more to the cave. I wished to speak to him but he pointed to his open mouth, and I saw that his tongue had been cut out, and he pointed to the castle and I knew who had done this thing. I stopped and put my hand on his shoulder and hung my head, in truth to hide my unchristian anger and my terror. But he looked behind at the castle again, and showed me with his hands that we should make haste, and I well understood his fear.

When we came to the cave, Guillaume showed me the creatures, but stared at me in shame. Because now, as I saw, they lived in their own filth, and the stink was a thousand times worse than before. There was a great deal of straw in their chamber but it was caked with ordure, and more was pushed in heaps against the wall and bars of the cage, with piles of bones and other matter from their food also. And the creatures were thin and covered in sores and wounds, from which a black substance ran thick. Then this good servant showed me by signs that Otto and his friends tortured the beasts for their pleasure.

Now, when I understood this, and as I looked upon their condition, I felt great pity for these living things; for, whatever else they were, they were that. And a torch was burning on the wall, and Guillaume pointed to it and to spears that were kept there in a rack in case they were needed against the creatures, and to all the straw on the floor and in heaps; and I understood his sad but merciful plan.

So Guillaume took a spear down and took it to the bars of the cage, and I looked at the creatures and their eyes of night and I shook again and knelt down at God's mystery and prayed for them.

But as I knelt there came a shout from the door at my back and Otto and his friends ran down the steps with their swords before them, and Otto was laughing. But though he laughed his face was red in his fury and he said:

"Halt, Cousin monk. My father gave leave for no mercy killing, as I recall, and it is my property now that you come meddling with, you and this treasonous servant. And if I know right, a man may defend his property." And his eyes blazed and he lifted his weapon above his head to strike me.

Now I am certainly no man of courage or of war, and I fell on my knees before him. But at that moment Guillaume ran to the door of the creatures' cage and took his key from his pouch and fitted it in the lock. When he saw what his servant meant to do, Otto cursed and hurled his sword at Guillaume's back, and Guillaume screamed and fell down.

When at first Otto and his men had burst in, the creatures had crouched low at the back of their cage, but now as Guillaume fell, they came to him yelping piteously, holding their hands to him through the bars. At that moment I found a little courage within my heart, whether because of the anger that came upon me or through the Lord who strengthens hearts I do not know, but I rose and said to Otto: "What would your father say to this? You have killed your servant."

But the boy only laughed and said: "Yes, and what would this worm have done to his master, while you delayed me with your begging?"

At that, he took one of his companion's swords and lifted it high and I waited trembling in prayer for my Maker, but from behind me now came a great roar, a terrible howl that surely none else under Heaven has heard, and the creatures themselves flung open their cage door, pushing back Guillaume's body, and I understood that the good servant had, by God's grace, unlocked the door before he died. I threw myself again on the floor, and now I would know who would grant me the greater mercy, the creatures of Sir Hugh or his son. The creatures ran at the three men, roaring and slashing the air with their claws as they went. Straight away one of the men ran back up the steps, but the beast near him caught his foot and dashed him against the wall, as a man kills a rat. Otto's other companion stood white and shaking, unable to move, and the second giant drove his claws into his breast and raked him on the stone floor like a carcass at a market, until he was rent in two.

Then the creatures turned towards Otto, but though his eyes were wide with terror at their might and fury, the boy did not run but remained steadfast. He raised his sword to them, and one of them slashed its claws at his throat but he stood back, and the claws did not touch him; but he took his sword in both hands and pierced the creature's side, and the poor beast fell to the floor holding his wound, and blood like tar spilled on the ground.

At this I heard a great noise that seemed it would crack the earth, a terrible howling and screaming from the other beast as he saw that his brother died. He leapt towards him and touched his body but the brother's life left him in a strange shaking and gaping of the mouth. And I saw that even Otto stood still a moment in awe, but quickly raised his weapon and ran at the living monster.

But with one stroke of his claws, the giant cut the boy down, and he fell back, his tunic split open at the chest and blood spilling forth. The creature stood and roared like thunder and strode toward Otto where he lay, while I could do no more than lie flat on the ground and cover my eyes with my hood and wait for the terrible revenge of this giant on his torturer, the slayer of his brother.

And indeed I heard yet more howling that was not of this world, though not a sound from Otto, and I waited; but nothing happened. Even as I shook, I lifted my head and opened my eyes, and saw something I hardly could believe: the great beast stood above his master's son, and roared and panted and swiped at him with his claws, but did not touch him. Otto stared at him, eyes wide as a wildcat's, and waited for the death blow, but it did not come. The creature only screamed once more into Otto's face, and turned and went to his dead brother, and sat down beside him, and began wailing as a child does, but with a noise like that of iron upon iron like to drive a man mad. And I looked and saw this giant, that could have killed Otto as an elephant crushes a fly, stroking his dead brother's body, rocking backwards and forwards, crying aloud in grief, and in truth I was utterly amazed.

At that moment I knew that all that Sir Hugh had believed about these creatures was true, and they were not brutes, but feeling and thinking beings as men are, and perhaps more besides. For though their power was great indeed, here was the one left alive grieving as to shake the heart for his brother, and when he could have slain his enemy he did not do so. And why not, if only for the love he bore Otto's father, his master? I did not dare to breathe, so full was I of astonishment and fear, and I did not know what I should do next.

But I thought also of Otto, who was sorely wounded, and how I might help him in the name of his father, as I am a man of Christian love, even though he had threatened my life. Yet I feared for myself also and dare not move, for I was not certain if the creature would spare me as it had the boy.

And this thought also troubled me: the monster was alive, and now free. It may be that it would leave me in peace and depart, but I asked myself: where would it go, and what terror would it cause the folk round about, and what then would they and their knights do to it? Our first idea of killing it out of mercy was far from my mind, now that I saw it in its great grief, even if I could do such a deed without Guillaume. But then there happened a marvellous thing: the servant moved and groaned, and pulled himself to the bars of the cage and sat up against them. He panted and held his side, where blood flowed, but he was living yet.

And, seeing this, the great beast, trembling in its misery, stood and came forward, and picked up the spear that Guillaume had dropped. I put my face again into the straw and prayed, but the creature did not harm us, and I looked and saw that it had turned the weapon so that the point was towards its own stomach, and the haft towards Guillaume.

But Guillaume pointed to the wound in his side and the blood there and shook his head to say that he was weak. He pushed the haft aside, and pointed to me, and nodded at me, and in horror I understood: he wished for me to do what the creature begged for.

Certainly it was the act that Guillaume and I had planned together to do, but I had thought that he alone would drive in the weapon.

But, obeying Guillaume, in whom he must have trusted above all other living men, the creature walked, in its strange rolling manner, towards me, holding out the spear. I stood, but I could not look at the beast, even at the claw that held out the haft. For now I had seen this creature in grief, and showing mercy and affection, and I did not believe I could kill it like a wounded dog.

But when I did look up it seemed to me that the thing cast back a look of pleading, and made signs as if to draw the spear into its body, and held it out again. And I saw how it longed for death. So I took the haft and held it, ready to strike, but straight away the creature rushed against the spearpoint, and the spear left my hands and I fell back, and the beast was writhing on the cave floor, howling, the ichor of its blood spilling from its belly. Yet it was not dying, and I rose and pulled the spear out, and prayed and with God's help thrust it in again with both hands, and purple and green and violet flesh and organs and more black blood burst onto the floor, and the creature howled and thrashed at the straw on the ground, until that and its breath ceased and it sank into peace. And I, like David, though a monk and a stranger to the arts of war, had killed a Goliath, though this giant, in the agony of its life, had begged that I would. But I do not believe that David shook and wept as I did then, nor knelt down in awe by the body of the mighty thing he had slain.

I thanked God aloud for His mercy, but as I spoke a great heaving and panting came upon me, and I would have swooned but that the Lord Himself gave me strength, as I surely believe. And at last I rose to my feet, and went to Guillaume to see his wounds. But

Guillaume pulled himself up on the bars of the cage and stood, and I saw that though he was weak he could walk, and he pushed me towards Otto, who lay even now flat on the ground. I lifted the boy's head, and as he groaned only a little I pulled him to his feet and took him to the steps and bade him stand there, and Guillaume came to us, leaning on the wall as he walked.

I left them a moment and went to both the creatures and gave the last rites and prayed for them, for I thought of what Sir Hugh would have wished.

Now as Otto was the more sorely wounded I took his arm and put it around my shoulders and pulled him up the steps to the door. Guillaume went to the torch on the wall and took it down and followed limping behind us; and at the top of the steps he turned and cast the torch back into the chamber. And I saw the straw catch quickly where it was dry and the flames ran to the piles of old straw and bones, and to the cloth hangings, and began at the strange giant chairs and table, and I hoped we had done right, but I turned and went from that place, with Otto leaning against me.

We went along the path back to the castle. I pulled the boy, and Guillaume followed as best he could, and as we limped I did not look back upon the fire, as Lot did not look back, because I thought that the consumption and forgetting of that place and the poor wretches that had been kept there was best for all. And the servants of the manor, seeing smoke, ran to put out the flames but I shouted after them to stand back from the fire and wait. For, I said, the flames were fierce and all those inside the cave were already dead, and they should only make sure the fire did not spread among the trees.

When we came near the end of the path, I went to a tree and knelt for a while, for I trembled again, this time it seemed beyond controlling. But I mastered myself, and prayed there for the souls of the men who had died, and even for the creatures, and that my Lord's son Otto might yet live.

At the castle, I gave the boy into the care of his servants and bade one of them fetch a surgeon. In his quarters, I gave Guillaume water and washed and bound his wound, which praise God was not as deep as had first appeared, for Otto's sword had cut his side as it had struck him, but not pierced the flesh as far as it might, though he had bled mightily and was weak.

And when the fire was finished I went again to the cave to make sure that nothing remained of the creatures, or the things they had with them in their cage, or any other sign of them. The few strange bones of the beasts that had not been consumed, I took and buried. The bodies of Otto's two companions were burnt almost to ashes, and I left those.

I stayed at the castle for a few days and helped to care for Guillaume and Otto while the surgeon tended them. The boy had his father's strength and though his wound was severe, he seemed like to recover. When he was strong enough I reminded him that he had tried to kill me, but said that I would tell no one of it, so long as he kept to a story that I had already made Guillaume understand. I told Otto that I would report to my Lord Abbot and the Sheriff that some wild animals that Sir Hugh had kept had broken loose, and that when Otto and his friends had bravely tried to cage them again, with help from Guillaume and my poor self, the friends had been killed and Otto had been attacked and wounded. Then a fire had started from the torches on the walls and consumed everything. I admonished Otto, as I had Guillaume, to agree to this story, in order to keep Sir Hugh's secrets, as he had heartily wished. I said that in this manner he must explain the deaths of his companions to their kinfolk, which task I gladly left to him.

May God forgive me for these untruths, but I may certainly claim I made them in good faith, to protect Sir Hugh and his son from the evil talk there would surely have been about them if we had spoken truly. And certainly, I may confess here, I wished to protect myself. For I knew well what my brother monks, as well as all the world, would think of me if I tried to tell the truth of Sir Hugh's monsters, and all that I had done at his behest.

Though he was weak, Otto grinned at me, as though now I was as much an evil-doer as he for lying, but he said he would keep to that story also.

When Otto was strong enough so that the surgeon let him stand, I told him that I must leave and return to my duties, and assured him that I would come again as often as I could, faithfully as his father had charged me. And, while I was absent, Guillaume would always be by his side and he must put his trust in him, for he was a good servant. I warned my new Lord that he must not again ill-treat Guillaume, for he was under my protection, and again if he treated the man well, Guillaume would be a boon to him as he had been to his father. And though Otto raised his lip, I had faith that there was somewhat less rage and madness in him now, after his battle, and perhaps he would think on the mercy that his father's poor creature had shown him, and the deaths of his friends that his recklessness had caused, and with his responsibilities he would become a man, and remember the good ways of Sir Hugh.

Guillaume saddled my horse and I bade him farewell. I grieved to leave him with a master who had treated him so ill, and yet I had in mind the love I still bore the boy's father and the promise I had made the good knight to care for his son, for I could think of no better servant to watch over him than Guillaume. So I begged this steadfast man to forgive Otto even the great wrongs he had done him, in remembrance of Sir Hugh, and to serve and care for the boy as well as he might, and to watch that he did not fall again into danger or evil ways. I entreated him to come for me as he had at the beginning if any unhappiness should befall him or his master, and I charged him that he was the keeper of the manor's secrets, and to guard them with his life. And though I saw the dread and sadness in the poor servant's heart, he bowed his head and I knew that he understood.

Then I rode on my way to Angelsbury, with many strange thoughts, and as great sorrow as wonder in my heart.

In private, I have thought many and many times of those two poor creatures, not least the one who died at my own hand, and asked myself again what they truly were. And I have prayed for understanding and searched secretly and diligently in many books, so far to no avail, so that even now I cannot answer. Were they men, or kin to men, and of the race of Adam as we are? This I cannot believe. For with their great size, scales, long teeth and eyes of ebony, they were not like any men known, even the strange races that some tell of, who live in the far regions of the world. And in truth, they were not demons either. For what demon would abide to live caged, in filth and misery, for so long as they did? And what demon may be slain by a sword or a spear? And neither were they animals. For what animals show love and mercy and intelligence, as Sir Hugh and I also perceived in them?

I think again and again on these things, and not out of simple curiosity. For there is a terrible mystery here, one that disturbs my heart and assails my mind as it must any Christian man's: if these creatures were intelligent, and had compassion, and were like men in so many ways, and yet were not of the race of Adam, but were not devils of Hell nor animals either, then of what race were they? And if we share this world with other creatures that are intelligent and have souls but are not men as we are, then why does Holy Scripture not tell us so? Were they with Adam in the Garden of Eden? Or did they have their own Creation? Did Christ die for them also? What was God's purpose in Sir Hugh's discovery of them, and all these things that I saw and took part in?

These are thoughts that burn me with confusion, and I cannot bear them, and yet I dare speak of them to no-one. But also I do not think it is right that the knowledge of these events should die with me and be lost forever. So I put up my papers in a secret place, that no man may read them but I, until an age comes that is more secure in its faith, and better understands the purposes of God. For I fear that these are not questions that any man, let alone my poor self, has faith enough to answer in these fallen times; and knowledge of such things as I have seen may cause men of less wisdom than the good Sir Hugh de Villiers even to doubt the Lord their Maker, to Whom all is known and in Whom, at the last, we cannot choose but put our trust. Amen.

David Penn *has previously published fiction in the magazines* Midnight Street *and* Whispers of Wickedness, *and poetry in the magazines* Magma *and* Smith's Knoll. *He lives in London where he also works, as a librarian.*

Three Bodies

Cam Rhys Lay

I. An Unwelcome Reception

When I exited the carriage I'd hired and walked through the ornately decorated front door of the gatehouse, a man in a fancy waistcoat greeted me from behind a wooden podium. I'd heard stories about the Gardens at Erith Bay, but since I was just common riff-raff and neither a) nobility, nor b) a merchant with gold tumbling out of her ass, I'd never actually been inside.

"Madam, may I help you?" the man at the podium said. He spoke with the practised courtesy his job required, but I could sense his poorly veiled disgust. He glanced over his shoulder at the Kallanbori guard who stood – at the ready – to chuck this little she-dwarf back out on the street from whence she'd came.

I couldn't quite see over the podium so I stood slightly to the side as I spoke to the man. "I'm here to see Lord Holdsclaw."

"And who might I tell him is here to visit?"

"Master Serafina Nicoletto."

"And the Lord is expecting you... *Master*?"

I nodded. He pulled a call bell from behind his podium, and a dark-skinned boy of twelve years or so, dressed all in white, came running. The greeter passed my name to the boy and he ran off again.

While I waited, a pale old man dressed in fancy

robes – his face swollen and red from drink – came in off the street with three young girls in tow. They looked like they were the right age to be the man's granddaughters.

They were not the man's granddaughters.

The greeter bowed deeply to the old man. "My Lord," he said and the wrinkled lecher walked through.

"A classy group of patrons you've got here," I said, when the old man had gone.

He put his hands behind his back and tilted his head up a little bit – as if he needed any help to look down at me. "Pardon the intrusion, but precisely what are you a *Master* of?"

Punching ass-hats like you in the balls.

"Inspector," I said, and displayed my Guild medal.

"Fascinating. I had no idea that a woman could be an inspector. Much less one of your," he looked me up and down, "...*attributes*."

"What's your name?" I said.

"Colby Clement, at your service." He bowed in mockery. "Why do you ask?"

"No reason, really." Just me keeping track of the people on my shit list.

The boy came running back. "Lord Holdsclaw will see you now," he said. "I will take you to him."

II. The Job

Erith Bay wasn't a real bay and the Gardens at Erith Bay weren't real gardens. *The Gardens* was a private club that sat on an inlet of the river where the rich and powerful of the capital could spend their leisure time when the estates outside the city, which might take two days or more to reach by carriage, were too much hassle. Here the elite could enjoy the good life – orgies of food and wine, an army of servants from the provinces – behind guarded walls that kept the misery of the rest of the city out of sight and mind.

"Lord Holdsclaw's cottage is one of the largest in the Gardens," the boy who accompanied me said. The word *cottage* was used just to sound quaint; I could see even the smallest of the houses here was three floors with enough room to comfortably house its owner and a dozen or two of his closest friends.

"Do you know Lord Holdsclaw?" I said.

"Only a little."

"I'm sure the other servants on the property gossip."

"I'm not much one to spread rumors, m'lady."

"Nothing will spread if I tell no one." I handed him a few coppers and he seemed to consider my offering as we walked side-by-side through a path lined with manicured topiaries.

"Well, Lord Holdsclaw is rich," he said at last.

"Aren't they all here?"

"Yes, but he is particularly rich. It is said he first made his fortune in silk, while still a boy, after the wars in the west opened up the trade routes to Lanzhao. But he truly became one of the richest men in the Empire only recently – through the production and sale of military supplies during the Uprising."

I pretty much knew all of this already. "Anything else?"

"No. Not really. Only that every lady in the city is in love with him."

It wasn't long before I saw firsthand what he meant. We crossed an enormous lawn to a massive stone manor and said our farewells. I knocked on the door.

Lord Bieron Holdsclaw himself, not a servant, answered, wearing a casual but expensive looking tunic and breeches, and he bid me enter. He was well past fifty, but his age just seemed to make him look more distinguished. Even as it was, having no interest in men, I still couldn't help but stare at his jaw line.

"It is so good to make your acquaintance," he said when we'd entered the sitting room. "Master Nicoletto: the talented lady inspector."

"You forgot *dwarf*." He looked at me, a question. "The talented lady *dwarf* inspector."

He smiled at my remark. "Perhaps. But still there is a kind of loveliness to you nonetheless. Your wonderful red hair, for instance." There was no irony in his voice. He really was a charmer. "May I?" he said and reached his own hand out for mine. I gave it to him and he kissed it. I resolved to never wash my hand again. "Can I have the servants bring you anything to drink? Wine perhaps?"

I wasn't usually one to turn down drink, but I was getting uncomfortable with all this flattery and kind attention. "No thank you," I said. "So what can I help you with? The message I received was somewhat sparse on details."

He sat down in one of the plush chairs that lined the wall. "My daughter. I'm worried about her."

"How so?"

"It's a man she's fallen in with."

"Tell me more."

"His name is Gar Mallott. He claims to be the son of a wealthy Altinian merchant and a veteran, come to the capital to make his own fortune now that the war's up."

"Why do you say *claim*? Do you have reason not to believe him?"

"Nothing solid. But the man does not give me a good feeling. There is something – how to say – *uncouth* about him."

"And your worry?"

"That he wishes to marry Shandra for my fortune."

"And a considerable fortune it is, if I've heard correctly. The war was good to you."

Holdsclaw grunted something unintelligible and frowned in such a way as to dismiss my comment.

I went on. "Does a well-bred girl born of your blood not have other things besides fortune to offer a man? Why do you fear the worst?" If she was half as attractive as her father...

"Shandra is no beauty. Nor, if I am honest, is she particularly clever. But I love her more than anything."

"Fair enough. Still, if my knowledge of the laws are correct, since you are a lord, she cannot marry without your consent anyway."

"If I refuse her I'm afraid she might take more drastic measures."

"Like do harm to herself?"

"No. But she might run away with him. I only have one child, you see."

"If this Gar is a fraud only after gold, how would running away benefit him?"

"He would not have legal rights to my fortune without marriage, but Shandra still has considerable money of her own. An inheritance from her uncle. Not a vast sum, but not a terrible consolation prize for a lowly thief."

"And so, what would you like me to do?"

"Follow up on this man. See what you can discover. If his story checks out and his intentions are true then so be it. But if not, then perhaps you can find me something more substantial to bring to my daughter regarding the man's deceitfulness."

We went over the logistical details: Gar's address in the capital, a basic description of him, my fees. I told him I'd send out feelers to contacts I had in the West, but that I'd see what I could dig up more locally over the next couple days.

"I'm sorry I didn't have a chance to meet your associate, Mr Nob," he said, as I was preparing to leave. "I'd heard the two of you were inseparable."

"Unfortunately my partner is ill at the present moment," I said. "A bad cold. Besides, I don't really need protection here, do I?"

"Yes, I suppose that's right. Still, I was looking forward to beholding such a renowned fighter."

I wanted to laugh, but didn't. Instead I simply bowed and saw myself out. On the way through the gatehouse, Colby gave me a snide smile. I would've loved to slap that expression off his face, but I had more important things to take care of at the moment.

III. Unrequited Affections

At the aviary, I sent a message to the Guild office in Altinus, to check on this Gar Mallott and get back to me as soon as possible. I included in the note Gar's name, the supposed name of his father, as well as the description Lord Holdsclaw had given me. Corresponding via pigeon was pretty much the least reliable thing one could do; even when sending multiple birds, there was a fifty percent or greater chance the message wouldn't get to its desired recipient and then a fifty percent or greater chance I wouldn't get the reply. Still, if we waited for the more reliable forms of communicating, Shandra Holdsclaw would be married and swollen with Gar's child before we knew anything.

I'd decided that over the next day or two, I would also pay a visit to an old acquaintance of Nob's and mine here in the capital by the name of Percel Callowsway. Percel had once been a wealthy merchant who had done a lot of business in Altinus. He'd fallen on hard times, but I thought there might be some chance he knew something about Gar or his family.

For now though, I'd head back to the office and Nob and I would pay Gar a visit. I made my way north, through the maze of New Kallanboro's shanties and toward the docks. The boat taxi wasn't the most direct way back to my office in Brogan's Alley, but it was a nice day to be on the water and, more importantly, it gave me an excuse to be "just passing by" Lila's house.

The last time I saw Lila, she'd told me that I was cruel and ugly and that she never wanted to see me again, but we'd both been drunk so I was pretending I hadn't heard or she hadn't meant it or both. Even if we'd both been sober, I'm not sure if I'd have been able to stay away. It was probably bad news for a woman like myself to get involved with a girl who was little more than half her age and married to a rich and powerful merchant who could probably have me assassinated without too much trouble, but as I'd been saying for a long time: *the heart wants what it wants*.

When I got to Lila's, I went around back to the stable to make sure that her husband's favorite riding horse was gone, and then walked to the other side of the house to toss a pebble at the second-story window of Lila's study. There was no telling if she was home, but when she was, she spent nearly all of her time in that room reading through those inane romantic epics that must have cost her husband a fortune. I waited for a minute and threw another pebble. I began hating myself a little. What was I doing here? Didn't I have any self-respect? If she didn't want to see me again then that was her loss, the bitch.

All these thoughts vanished the instant the luxurious green drapes were pulled back and my love's face materialized in the window. It would be inaccurate to say that I'd forgotten what she looked like, but even still, I had a habit of being surprised by her loveliness every time I saw her. Lila was no beauty by traditional standards. Her ears stuck out from her head and her eyes were a little too close together. Nonetheless, she had that ordinary kind of beauty that youth provides as well as a kind of cleverness in her eyes and expression that I found totally alluring. And, of course, any time I saw her I was reminded of those wondrous, holy, magical things she could do with her mouth, her tongue, her hands, all in unison, as if she were a virtuoso musician, playing the human instrument of my body.

She opened the window and stuck her delicate, pale neck out. "What are you doing here, Sera?" she said in what was somehow both a whisper and a shout. "I told you I didn't want to see you anymore."

"Can we just talk for a minute?" I gave her my best pleading look.

She sighed. "Fine, we'll go for a walk. Meet me at the corner. I don't want the servants to see you."

She came out wearing a simple yet elegant wool dress that flaunted all of her youthful contours and made me want to stop everything and beg her – grovel before her – to come with me to the nearest boarding house where we could spend a few days naked in each other's embrace.

We walked mostly in silence, into the Imperial Park not far from Lila's house. It was a lovely autumn day and many of the rich of the city rode through the wooded park in open carriages. In a clearing to our left, artisans were constructing some kind of monument that would supposedly be unveiled on the one-year anniversary to the end of the Uprising in the North, in which tens of thousands on both sides of the conflict had perished. When we walked by a trio of young men one of them called out after Lila, "A nice pet you have there, m'lady." I decided not to take offense. In my thirty-eight years I'd heard far worse.

"I thought you said you wanted to talk," Lila said. "Talk then."

I cleared my throat. "I suppose I just wanted to say sorry for what I said. About you... and Caius. I didn't mean it." This wasn't true, but if the lie would get me back in Lila's good graces, then so be it. Lila's husband, Caius, was a brute and arrogant and I wanted Lila to leave him. Not just for my sake, but her own as well.

"Well thank you," she said. "I'm glad you realise how terrible you were being. Nonetheless, I don't think we should see each other any longer. I've been thinking a lot on my marriage and how can I expect my husband to treat me well when I deceive him and betray him at every turn?"

This was garbage and we both knew it. Caius had been beating on the girl since long before I ever set eyes on her. Still, Lila was stubborn if she was anything, and I knew there was nothing I could say to change her mind.

IV. Sera's Partner Gets a Skirt

When I got back to the office I went upstairs to Nob's apartment, across the hall from my own, to check in on my partner.

I knocked and he told me to enter in his usual jovial voice. I walked in and saw that, though Nob wore his usual grey tunic, he was standing in a kind of half squat with his legs far apart and was naked from the waist down. Given my low vantage point, I couldn't help but glimpse his manhood – a long, but disproportionately skinny serpent, the colour of a bruise despite its owner's otherwise light complexion. I turned away in horror.

"Nob!" I shouted and stared at the wall. "Why aren't you wearing pants?"

"Hi Sera," he said, like nothing was out of the ordinary. "It's this rash all over my groin, see?"

"No. I don't want to see."

"It feels so much better without my pantaloons

rubbing up against it. In fact, my fever's down and, with my pants off, I almost feel like new."

"Well, that's really helpful." I walked in a few more steps, using my hand to shield my eyes from the view. I picked up a chair, and faced it away from Nob before sitting down. "A lot of productive business you're going to get done without your pants."

"The healer said it will only be another day of applying the salve before the pain goes away completely."

"This is what happens when you go see cut-rate whores. Can we talk about the Holdsclaw job?"

"She was hardly cut-rate, Sera... But sure, let's talk."

"Can you at least throw a blanket on top of yourself or something?"

"Even a blanket hurts. You see the rash isn't so much on the sword as on the stones and this whole surrounding area, here. See—"

"I. Don't. Want. To. See."

"Okay, Sera. Have it your way."

With my back still to him, I told him about the case and we jointly decided to pay our man Gar a visit. If we left within the hour, we'd be able to get to his house by dusk. First though, I went downstairs to the nearest clothier where I purchased for Nob one of those Niffleheimen man-skirts. When he tried it on, he told me that it was still uncomfortable, but I didn't care. He was going to have to deal with the pain. Let this be a lesson for him.

V. The Man in Question

Gar lived in a row house in Bluefield, roughly an hour by carriage from our office, that looked to have once been painted a bright yellow, but that through time had faded and cracked into a dirty, decrepit cream.

Bluefield wasn't the worst neighborhood in the capital, but it also wasn't the best, and the house did not immediately shout "son of a wealthy merchant".

Nob and I didn't have to search for our man long. Someone fitting Gar's description (tall and thin, brown hair tied back in a bun, blue eyes, handsome "in a boyish way") was standing out front arguing with another, older man, when we arrived. I noted how the man I believed to be Gar had an unnaturally high and effeminate voice.

I told Nob we should hang back beside a row of hedges, close enough to eavesdrop, but not close enough to draw the men's attention from each other. From what I could glean by the two men's argument, the older was a wine merchant and the two were fighting over some money Gar allegedly owed him. I was happy to have us stand by, out of the fray, and watch, until the wine merchant took Gar by the collar and looked to be on the verge of strangling him. I nodded to Nob – barely able to look at my ridiculous, skirted partner – and he stepped in to separate the two feuding men.

"Ho-ho, calm down my friend," Nob said to the wine merchant, easily holding him at bay with one arm.

"Let me go," the wine merchant said.

"So you can strangle this young man over here?" Nob said.

"This *young man* is a scoundrel and a degenerate who owes me four crowns for the casks of wine I've brought him last week."

"Much of the stuff was spoiled," Gar said. "You were lucky I gave you the two crowns I did." Every time he said anything I was surprised all over again by that squeal of a voice.

"Spoiled? Then where is it?"

"I poured it out. It was stinking up my house."

"*Poured it out*... Bah! Down your throat."

"How about I pay the difference?" I said, stepping toward the three men. I pulled out a few coins from the purse Lord Holdsclaw had given me as advance against my expenses.

This seemed to appease the winemaker; he shrugged his shoulders. "If you wish," he said. "Although I advise you to watch yourself with whatever business you have with this deadbeat." He snatched the coins from my hand and walked back to his cart.

"That was generous of you," Gar said, looking with measuring eyes at Nob and me, "but you shouldn't have paid such a man."

"It seems as if, for the sake of your neck, someone had to," I said.

"I would have been fine. I've seen my share of battle."

"Veteran?" I said.

At this he perked up. "Rode at the front of the column that broke the Alliance lines at Xanthas. I will never forget that day: the sound of the war drums, the smell of blood in the air..." His expression changed again, now into a melancholy frown – as if the memory simultaneously conjured up both pride and heartbreak.

Nob, who was out of Gar's field of vision, gave me a doubtful raise of his eyebrows. While Gar was a pretty thing with an earnest face that immediately made you like him, he didn't look to be much of a fighter. If an old winemaker could best him, it didn't seem too likely that he would have done well against the Domani hoards.

"In any event," Gar said, shaking himself out of his mood, "I don't believe we've met."

"I'm Serafina Nicoletto and this is my associate Nob." We'd tossed around the idea of using a variety of different cover stories, but ultimately decided that honesty might serve us best in this case. It was possible that Gar was telling the truth about everything. If he wasn't, he might be more liable to slip up if he thought we were on his side. "We've been hired to look into you a little bit and would just like to talk with you for a few minutes."

"And who might your employer be?" he said, defensive now.

"Who do you think?" I said.

He narrowed his eyes as if we'd done him an injustice by letting the idea of the man cross his mind. "Holdsclaw."

I nodded.

"I thank you for your generous contribution earlier, Madam. But I don't have anything else to say to a pair of Holdsclaw's lackeys. He hates the idea of any man, other than one he hand selects, being with his daughter." Gar turned past Nob and started walking back toward the house's front door.

"Wait," I said and he looked over his shoulder at me. "What you say about Lord Holdsclaw may be correct, but *we* just want to figure out the truth. If you speak with us and everything checks out, I promise we'll put in a good word for you."

He gave this some thought. "Come in," he said finally.

The house was a simply furnished and decorated place with a large wooden table and bench on one side of the sitting room. On the other side was a single chair as well as a shelf, which held a polished Imperial breastplate and sword, along with an Imperial red cape and several other pieces of military regalia.

Nob and I sat down on the bench, Gar in the chair. I hoped Gar didn't notice that Nob sat with his legs spread wide: someone with the proper angle could peer right up his woollen skirt.

He brought us water (we understood why he didn't

have wine): a large glass for Nob and "a small cup for the small lady".

"So if you don't mind, can you tell us a little bit about yourself?" I said.

"What do you want to know?"

"Just the general stuff: where you're from, why you're in the capital... Whatever you think we should know."

Gar repeated the same details Lord Holdsclaw had told us: son of a merchant, veteran from the war, come to the capital to make a name for himself.

"Quite a few years ago I used to work for Lord Calembere," Nob said. "I believe he settled down in Altinus... I'd guess that a young man from a well-appointed family like your own might have made his acquaintance. You ever, by chance, meet the man?" I could tell that Nob was talking out of his ass, likely to try and catch Gar being dishonest. Whenever Nob was lying, he always twisted and untwisted his long grey mustache, just like he was doing now. In all likelihood, there was no such man as "Lord Calembere".

"I'm sorry, but I've never heard of him," Gar said.

"Oh, that's too bad," Nob said, "he really is a remarkable man: a brilliant scholar of the ancient texts, the finest archer I've ever seen and quite the competent juggler as well."

I fired an expression of displeasure in Nob's direction but he wasn't looking at me.

"Out of curiosity," I said, "do you have any personal items or papers that verify your identity? A letter of introduction from your father to someone here in the capital, perhaps?" I knew that such things could obviously be forged, but they might lend some amount of credibility to his story.

Gar went into the adjacent room and returned with several official-looking documents, which he handed to me. They appeared to be military service records, listing Gar's full name (*Garvin Mallott*), highest rank

(*Lieutenant*) birth year (*1,873rd Year After the Fall*), city of origin (*Altinus*) and commendations (*Bravery in battle at Corolainin and Xanthas*). The documents appeared legitimate, but I handed them to Nob, since he had actually served with the Redcloaks long ago. "What do you think?"

"They're real. This is the Grand Councillor's seal right here," he said, pointing to the wax mark on the document's lower left-hand corner.

"And you've shown these to Lord Holdsclaw?" I said.

"Of course I have," Gar said.

"Do you then, good sir, have any idea why he still doubts your identity?" Nob said.

"I have no idea what goes on in that man's twisted mind."

Just then a woman walked into the house. She was tall, with broad shoulders and a face that looked exactly like Lord Holdsclaw's save for it being younger and framed by long dark-brown hair. Unfortunately for Shandra Holdsclaw, this face, so becoming for a man, didn't have quite the same effect on a woman.

"Darling," Gar said and stood up. He went over and kissed the girl passionately on the lips, only stopping when she pushed him away. There was something undoubtedly awkward and theatrical about this gesture of affection.

Shandra wiped her face of Gar's saliva and gestured to us. "These are the people my father hired, aren't they? Why are you talking to them?"

"It's true your father hired us," I said, "but all we're after is the truth."

"They've promised to put in a good word with your father," Gar said.

"Assuming everything checks out," I said.

"It will," he said.

"It doesn't matter what you say to him," Shandra

said. "My father has already made up his mind that I shouldn't be with Gar."

"Despite your father's faults, he loves you," I said.

"He may think he does, but he's incapable of loving anything but himself and his money and his 'legacy'. Why else would he be trying so hard to keep me away from the one person in this world who makes me happy?"

"Maybe he thinks he's protecting you. Or maybe he *does* have another reason," I said. "But what I can say to you with certainty is that Nob and I are only interested in making sure we find the truth."

"That's good to know," she said. I couldn't discern whether she was being sarcastic.

"I think we have the information we've come for today, but with your permission, we will return if we need anything further?"

Shandra nodded noncommittally. Nob and I stood up to leave. I wanted to talk to Shandra, but I couldn't do it with Gar around.

VI. A Surprise Visit

Nob and I spent the following morning in the office discussing what our next move should be. Mercifully, Nob had started wearing pants again. We both agreed that it seemed unlikely the military records were forgeries. This meant that in all likelihood *Gar Mallott* existed. Still, there was no guarantee that our man hadn't stolen both the records as well as the military regalia. And even if he was *whom* he claimed, that still didn't mean that his motives were *what* he claimed.

We had just concluded that we'd go talk to Percel Callowsway to see if he happened to know anything about Gar, when there was a frantic, violent knocking on the office door. Nob went through the other room to answer and then called me over.

When I saw who it was, I immediately became aware of the thumping sensation in my chest.

As far as I knew, Lila had never been to this part of the city before, let alone to my office. I was happy to see her, only not like this. Her face was puffy and her eyes were red from crying. I invited her in and had her sit down on the couch in the office to try and calm down. Nob pretended to not notice us. "What's wrong, Lye?"

"It's Caius," she said.

"Has he been beating you again?" She didn't show any outward signs of being hit, but maybe the bruises were under her clothes. I imagined her marvelous, pale body covered in green and purple marks. I had half a mind to send Nob to pay the bastard a visit.

"No," she said, "they've taken him away."

"Who?"

"The Redcloaks."

"Why would the Redcloaks take him?"

"I don't know," she said, still sobbing. She told me how very early that morning a dozen or more Imperial soldiers had burst into their house, knocking down their front door. They'd walked into the bedroom and one of the Redcloaks had punched Caius in the face with a gauntleted hand before dragging his unconscious body out onto the street. Several of the others had stayed to search the house, although for what, Lila didn't know. When she tried to ask them what this was all about, they only told her to stand aside, that her husband was a traitor.

"You'll help, won't you, Sera?" Lila said. "Find out what's going on?"

I was almost certain that Caius deserved whatever was happening to him, but I couldn't say no to Lila. I told Nob to stay with Lila for the morning and then, if

Lila was holding up alright, to go without me and pay Percel a visit. Nob agreed that this sounded like a good plan. I left the office and hired a carriage to take me to the center of the city.

The Redcloaks probably would have taken Caius to the Imperial jail next to the Capital Building. I'd done some work for the Grand Councillor's Office some years before the war and thought that I might be able to get some of my contacts to give me information. And so, after the three-hour journey to the Imperial Administration Office, I spent the remainder of the day talking to bureaucrats who directed me to yet other bureaucrats who directed me to some of the bureaucrats I'd started with. The evening bells had long since rung by the time I had some sense of what had happened.

Apparently an investigation had recently uncovered "evidence" of a number of imperial citizens in the capital who had, during the war, profited through secretly aiding the enemy and selling them supplies, weaponry, intelligence. Emperor Kaleb himself had ordered the arrests of at least a score of wealthy individuals around the city so that the alleged traitors could be brought in for questioning. If the accusations were correct, there was nothing I could do for Caius. He was pretty much screwed.

I got back to the office late in the night. The moment I opened the door, Nob ran up to me. "We need to talk," he said.

"Is Lila alright?"

"Yes. I put her to bed up in your apartment. It's just that I spoke with Percel."

"Oh." I was relieved. "How's he doing?"

"I think he's still bent about losing his fortune and his house. And he was drunk the entire time I was there. But, you know, he was fine."

"And did he have anything to say? Does he know anything about Gar?"

"He told me he'd never actually met Gar, but he knew of him, and he was quite familiar with the Mallott family and confirmed that they're exactly as we've been told: a well-respected merchant family out of Altinus."

"But..."

"Although Percel's never met Gar, he did know quite a lot *about* him—"

"Like?"

"That he was a great swordsman, a war hero... And that when he came back from the Battle of Xanthas he was never the same man."

"How so?"

"According to what Percel heard, the boy lost an arm, lost a leg, was more or less bedridden, and could barely speak a word."

I went upstairs into my bedroom where a single candle had nearly burned all the way down. In the dim candlelight, I could just barely see my beloved's peaceful face. Rather than wake her, I decided I'd just let her sleep. I hated the idea of leaving her again just as soon as I'd gotten back, but we had to get back to "Gar's" house. I had a feeling it was only a matter of time before something really bad happened.

VII. An Empty House

We hired a carriage and arrived back in Bluefield some time in the middle of the night. All the windows were dark at "Gar's" house, but this was to be expected given the hour. We went up the short walkway to the front door and Nob knocked three times. After a minute he knocked again.

When I noticed the high windows above the door

hadn't been shuttered, I had Nob stoop down so I could climb on his shoulders. Nob got back to his feet and held his lantern as high as he could while I, from atop my partner, peered through the window. Even with the lantern I could hardly see anything.

"Here, give me that," I said and took the lantern from him. The front room looked largely as I remembered, except I could just now make out a few articles of clothing, some papers, strewn upon the floor inside. I partially climbed down Nob's left side and then hopped to the ground. "Something's not right. Let's go inside."

"You know we're not supposed to do that, right Sera?"

I rolled my eyes. We'd done far worse. I picked the lock and we walked in.

Nob placed the lantern on top of the shelf in the front room. In addition to the items strewn about the floor, the first thing I noticed was that the sword and breastplate and cloak were gone.

Nob picked up a couple of the papers on the floor and started examining them next to the lantern.

"Anything interesting?" I said.

"Not really. Just some contract invoices for some provisions: wine, a few pounds of grain, two slabs of bacon."

I went up the creaky wooden stairs to the bedroom. Although I'd left the lantern downstairs, I could still get around by the moonlight that came in through the upstairs windows. The small bed was unmade and a chest of clothes lay open with a few pairs of stockings hanging halfway out. I noted that on the small table next to the bed, a nice porcelain vase stood undisturbed. It wasn't worth a fortune, but probably something that would have been taken in a break in.

"Looks like Gar left in a hurry," I said when I

rejoined Nob on the ground floor. He was examining a small scroll he had unrolled against the wall.

"Sera, what do you think of this?"

He handed me the scroll. It looked to be some kind of account ledger from the Imperial Bank of Alderia. In the corner of the document I saw the name *Bieron Holdsclaw*. From the dates in the ledger, the records looked to be a little less than two years old.

"Think this suggests some kind of money scheme or fraud on Gar's part?"

That would be my first instinct. But why then would he be looking at such old records? "I'm not sure," I said. "But I think tomorrow morning we need to pay Lord Holdsclaw another visit."

VIII. Return to Erith Bay

"Gone?" Lord Holdsclaw said. "What do you mean he's gone?"

It was early the next morning and Nob and I had just arrived back at Lord Holdsclaw's cottage. We were seated in the breakfast room; the windows offered us a lovely view of the flower garden, which encircled a manufactured pond. Holdsclaw was dressed just in a robe, open near the top so one could see the smattering of grey hairs that dotted his bronze, and still strong-looking, chest. For my part, after the previous night, I could barely keep my eyes open. Nob looked chipper as ever.

I'd just gotten done telling Holdsclaw everything: our visit with Shandra and "Gar" two days before, Nob's conversation with Percel, and the state we'd found the Bluefield house in the previous night. Something told me not to mention the bank records just yet.

"Some of his things were missing from the house. It

didn't look like a burglary, so my only guess is that he's gone somewhere."

"Shandra never returned home yesterday night," Holdsclaw said.

I'd suspected this might be the case. "Is this unusual behaviour for her?" I said.

"Of course it isn't usual. But I assumed she was just spending the evening with Gar – or rather, this man we know is not Gar – to punish me. But now..." He took a sip of his tea and stood up to look out the window, his face pointed away from us. When he placed his cup back down onto the saucer he called over one of his servants and asked him to bring two more cups for Nob and me.

"You know, Shandra was always far closer with her mother," Holdsclaw said and started in on a long, uninteresting story about an incident from Shandra's childhood. I tried my best to pay attention, but my own mind, sluggish already from lack of sleep, drifted to the previous night when Nob and I returned from Gar's house.

As soon as I'd walked into my apartment, I'd gone immediately to the bedroom where Lila was still fast asleep in my bed. It was only a few hours until dawn, when we'd leave for Holdsclaw's again, so I decided to just build a makeshift cot on my threadbare rug rather than get into bed with Lila. I tried to be as quiet as possible, but the moment I laid down on the floor, I heard Lila stir. "Is that you Sera?" she said.

I got up and crawled into the bed with her. I placed my chin upon her shoulder so that I could smell her neck, her hair. There was a kind of earthy aroma to her that wasn't exactly pleasant, but that I loved anyway. When I told her about Caius she started crying and it was then that she kissed me. I kissed her back and slowly my kisses descended down her face, her breasts, the tiny blond hairs that led from her abdomen past her navel to the thicker auburn foliage between her legs.

Afterwards, Lila didn't offer to reciprocate, but I didn't mind.

Lord Holdsclaw finished the tale after five minutes or so and gestured to Nob. "Is this your partner, I presume? You didn't introduce us."

"Sorry, yes," I said. By now the extra teacups had been brought. I hoped it was a strong brew. "This is Nob. Nob: Lord Holdsclaw."

"Lord Holdsclaw," Nob said and bowed slightly.

"My pleasure," Holdsclaw said.

"So any idea where they might have gone?" I said.

"No. I've already had my servants check the main house when Shandra didn't come home last night. Not that she would go there with Gar anyway... They could have gone anywhere, really."

I turned to Nob. "We should put the word out to the Guild. My fear is that Shandra could be in some danger."

"What kind of danger?" Lord Holdsclaw said.

"I don't know. Maybe none. But I worry that 'Gar' might have decided to run when he learned someone was looking into him, and that he might resort to something drastic now. Of course, I hope I'm wrong. We just need to find your daughter."

Holdsclaw seemed to be thinking to himself. "Well, come to think of it, it's possible that they could have gone to... We have a summer home just outside the city. I haven't been there for years, but we used to go there when Shandra's mother was still alive. Shandra always loved that place. And since I never go there, that might be someplace they would steal away to."

He gave us the location of the summerhouse. It wasn't as far as some of the lake estates outside the city, but it would still take a day by carriage. We could probably cut that time in half on horseback. Given my stature, I hated riding, but would, from time to time, ride with Nob on his horse, when the situation called for such a desperate action.

"We'll leave immediately," I said and turned to Nob. "We can notify the Guild on the way."

"Very well," Holdsclaw said. "Please report to me as soon as you return."

"We will. One more thing though before we leave."

"What's that?"

"Do you know why this Gar impostor might be interested in your bank ledger records?"

"Bank records?" he said. "What are you talking about?"

Nob produced the scroll and showed it to Holdsclaw. I studied the Lord's confused face as he examined the scroll. For the briefest instant, I thought I saw a flash, of something, before his expression returned from whence it came.

"I have no idea why this would have been at Gar's house. The only thing I can think of is that somehow Shandra left it by mistake."

"And why would Shandra have old bank records?"

"Despite her being a woman, I have been trying to teach her the family business and it's not uncommon for one of my associates or me to go over the various ledgers with her."

"Oh, I understand," I said. "Perhaps it's nothing then. We'll be on our way."

Nob and I each gave a courteous bow, but Lord Holdsclaw spoke again before we could make our exit. "Wait," he said. "I was just thinking of something. Upon further reflection I don't think Shandra would have gone to the summerhouse. It's too obvious and she would know I'd have someone look there. I think we should instead continue our search within the city. The last thing I want is for the two of you to spend two days riding off when that time could be better used here in the capital."

I stole a glimpse at Nob.

"Very well. You're paying," I said. "We'll send out word to the Guild and then start searching the city. We'll head back out to Bluefield to see if we can find any clues there."

As soon as we left the cottage and were back on the topiary-lined path to the gatehouse, Nob turned to me. "So we're still going out to this summerhouse, aren't we?"

Nob knew me well.

Maybe it was a bad thing for an investigator to be too curious and maybe that was why I lived and worked out of a decrepit building in Brogan's Alley and only drank cheap wine except when someone else was paying. But there was nothing to be done about it. I was who I was. I tried to do what my clients asked and to generally do my best by them. But I had an unwritten rule that all that went out the window when my clients hid the truth from me, tried to play me for a fool. And while I still wasn't sure what the truth was, I was sure that Holdsclaw wasn't telling it.

IX. Two Bodies

We took the first carriage we could find and told the driver to push the horses double-time back to the office in Brogan's Alley. I had Nob send out a message to the Guild and ready his horse, while I went upstairs to check in on Lila. On the table in the front room, I found the half-eaten remains of Lila's breakfast on one of my ceramic plates: the plucked stems of grapes, a small, white cheese rind, a piece of bread missing a chunk roughly the size of Lila's mouth. Lila sat across the room by the window brushing her hair. "How'd you sleep?" I said to her.

She had a piteous look on her face. "I don't know, Sera," she said. "I just can't stop thinking about Caius." Slowly, tears formed in her eyes and she began to quietly weep. "Poor Caius..."

Yes. Poor Caius. Forced to finally reap the nasty harvest he had sown through what was undoubtedly a lifetime of misdeeds. I took the brush from her and dragged the thing through her curls over and over. Eventually all her tears were spent.

"Did you finish whatever business you had with Nob?" she said after a time.

"No. I have to leave again."

"Now?"

I nodded.

She started up again with the weeping. "Sera... Don't leave me alone. Not now."

Her pleas were tempting, and I had the violent urge to undress, bring her back to the bedroom, and let our two bodies – hers wonderful, mine stunted and deformed – mingle indefinitely beneath the blankets. In this way, I thought – in our mutual ecstasy – might we temporarily shield ourselves from all knowledge of the cruel world beyond these walls.

A nice thought, but there was no time for any of that.

"I'll only be gone for a day, I think."

"A day?" she said as if I'd said a year. She closed her eyes tightly as if by doing so I'd vanish from existence. I loved Lila's youth. But the other side of her youthful body and exuberant spirit was this: youthful immaturity. Lila's life hadn't been perfect – far from it – but by most standards she lived a charmed existence and was used to getting her way.

"Please stay here," I said. I kissed her still-closed

eyelids and went downstairs. Nob had already gotten his horse ready.

Nob and I headed east toward the city gates. It quickly became apparent to me why, despite the slower speeds, I usually rode in carriages or wagons rather than with Nob on horseback. First, there was the endless jolting – up and down and up and down – such that after the first half hour of riding through the poorly maintained cobblestone streets of the capital, I felt as if I'd been repeatedly kicked in my head, my neck, between my legs. Then of course, there was the fact that I was faced with the constant choice of either loosely holding onto Nob and chancing the possibility of being thrown to my death, or else clinging to him tightly, my face in his back, and subjecting myself to his pungent mix of body odours.

Eventually, the sprawl of the city grew thinner, the buildings farther apart, until, save the occasional mansion estate, there were hardly buildings at all. Despite the smell of Nob still invading my nostrils, I noted that the tree-scented air seemed fresher out here.

The house was located on the banks of one of the Riffel's tributaries in the wooded hills an hour's ride from the city walls. By the time we drew near, it was quite late and extremely dark out – the moon and stars being covered over by clouds. We could see neither the house nor the address easily; however, the large stone arch out front that read *Holdsclaw* told us we must be in the right place. A faint light, perhaps from a single candle, flickered in one of the house's windows a hundred paces away.

"Let's walk from here," I said.

We left the horse and were halfway up the path when we heard a series of loud bangs and the sound of men shouting. A woman screamed; Nob and I started running toward the house. Nob's legs were longer so

he reached the front door first. Before he could grab
the door handle though, the heavy wooden door
swung open on its own, knocking my partner back.
On the other side of the doorway was a figure dressed
all in black, a scarf tied around his face such that the
only thing exposed were his eyes. He held a short
sword in his hand. Nob drew his own blade from its
scabbard and shifted his feet into a fighting stance. I
unsheathed my dagger, although knowing Nob, I
wasn't going to have to use it.

"Put the sword down, friend," Nob said.

The man in black didn't say anything. He seemed to
hesitate for a moment, unsure whether to run back the
way he'd come or stay and fight. Then, all at once, he
leapt at Nob swinging his sword downward in a wild,
desperate arc.

Nob expertly stepped aside, parried the blow and
countered with an effortless stroke that landed cleanly
in the space where his adversary's neck and right
shoulder met. Even in the dark of night I could see the
man's blood spray into the air.

Another scream sounded from within the house – I
recognized it as Shandra's voice now – followed by a
series of loud sobs. Nob and I ran into the house and
up the flight of stairs. At the top of the landing a
doorway opened into the room with the lit candle.
There, Shandra Holdsclaw sat on the floor shaking,
her hands and forearms covered in blood.

"M'lady, we're here to help," Nob said. "Is there
anyone else in the house?"

Shandra didn't answer. When we walked into the
room, we saw that there *was* someone else in the
house, only he was no longer amongst the living. The
man who claimed to be Gar Mallott lay on the floor,
the center of a growing oval of blackish liquid. A large
gash in his chest spouted irregularly, a dysfunctional
fountain.

Nob checked the other rooms to make sure there hadn't been a second intruder, and I went downstairs to check on Nob's assailant. Unfortunately for us (and even more unfortunately for the man in black), Nob was too competent a warrior. The single blow had been a fatal one. I removed the dead man's headscarf, trying not to get my fingers too messy. He was a young man – twenty-five maybe – with shoulder-length dark hair and an expression of surprise on his face. His short sword was the type of weapon that was a favorite of assassin types, but from the looks of him, it was easy to imagine him as just some poor idiot who thought he'd make quick gold by doing what sounded like an easy job.

I went back upstairs and tried to get Shandra cleaned up as best as I could with the basin of water in the corner. Nob and I agreed that despite the hour, we should return to the city immediately.

Shandra and Gar had ridden a small, two-horse carriage to the summerhouse, so on the return to the city, I drove the carriage and Shandra sat beside me up front. Nob rode alongside us on his horse. The whole ride back, I tried to keep talking to Shandra – about myself, about her childhood, about anything I could think of. She hardly said a word, but I kept on talking. I wanted to distract her from the fact that right in back we were hauling two bodies: that of her lover and that of his killer. I was fairly sure that fake Gar had never loved Shandra in any genuine way. He'd had other motives for why he'd tried to woo her. Still, I knew better than most that such things were irrelevant for how Shandra felt now, her world toppling down. I felt a tenderness somewhere between my heart and my guts. I pitied her – and pitied myself too.

X. Two Letters

We arrived back at the office around mid-morning. It had been just after dawn broke that we'd returned within the city walls, but we'd spent several hours first dropping Shandra off at her cousin's house in the Phaidonian District and then taking the two bodies to the nearest constable's office. We'd asked Shandra if she'd wanted to be brought to her father, but she'd refused.

"Why would I want to see the man who had my beloved killed?" she said. She wasn't really crying any more, but she spoke in an eerie monotone; all the emotion had been drained from her.

"How do you know your father was behind it?"

"He couldn't stand the idea of Gar and me being together."

"A man like Gar," I said, "may have had many enemies. I told you already that he wasn't really the man he claimed to be..."

"What does it matter, his name?" she said vacantly.

I didn't doubt that Lord Holdsclaw had sent the assassin. It was more that I doubted the motive could be as simple as Shandra made it out to be. There was still the matter of the bank ledgers.

After we dropped off Shandra and the bodies, it was still another hour back to the office. I'd barely slept in two days. It was only the thought of Lila in my bed that kept me from falling asleep in the wagon.

When Nob and I arrived, I ran ahead of my partner into the office and up the stairs to my quarters. "Lila," I called from the front room, but no one responded. "Lila?"

I went into the adjacent room where the bed was and saw that it was neatly made up, with a single sheet of parchment on top of the pillow.

"Everything okay, Ser?" Nob called from the hallway separating our two apartments.

"Yeah," I said, as my eyes started to scan the letter. "Lila left."

"Oh."

Lila had terrible penmanship. I realised I'd never actually seen anything she'd written before. Surprising, seeing as we'd had a secret affair.

Dear Sera,

This morning I sent a courier boy over to the house and received word that Caius's trial took place last night and that he was found unanimously guilty of treason. He is to be executed in two days by way of the headsman's axe.

It is a strange thing that, though I often despised my husband during our marriage, upon learning of his impending death, I realise that a part of me loves him very much and the thought of his death – a death that I even wished for at times – gives me not joy, but great sadness. I cannot stay in the capital any longer and have made arrangements to travel south to my aunt and uncle's house for a time. I don't know if I will ever return to this city, but I feel that I will likely never see you again. Now is my chance to start anew – away from my terrible marriage, but also away from the sinful relations that we two had between us. Despite the yearnings of my flesh, I know it is unnatural for us two women to be together. Please do not hate me for not waiting to say farewell to you in person. It is better this way.

Goodbye,
L

I sat down on the floor and read the letter a few more times, trying to find some hidden consolation amongst the words. There wasn't any. Part of me wondered whether Lila would have viewed our relations as somehow less "unnatural" had I her same height and proportions. Lila would deny it, but I wasn't so sure.

When I'd committed the letter to memory, I took off my boots, got up on the bed and buried my head in the pillow. Was that the smell of her hair again or was I just imagining now? Did it matter? She was gone and I was being pathetic. Thankfully, this only lasted a few hours before Nob knocked on the door to my apartment.

"What is it?"

He came in from the hallway and then walked into the room I was in. "A letter from the aviary," he said.

"That was fast. What does it say?"

"Here. You read it."

I sat up in bed and wiped the sorry tears from my face. I took the small scroll from Nob. It was written in the usual terse sentences of the Guild office.

Confirmed existence of wealthy Mallott mercantile family. Confirmed existence of Gar Mallott. HOWEVER, also confirmed Gar served in war and was maimed at Xanthas. Now crippled. Also dumb. Interviewed Mallott family members and gave description of suspect. Based on description, family strongly believes your impostor to be best friend of Gar from Imperial Army named Torvis Burdon. Burdon said to be unstable, mayhaps even touched by madness. According to Mallott family, Burdon obsessed with idea that many Imperial casualties at Xanthas result of traitorous Alliance collaborators who aided Northern Alliance during war. Burdon last seen six months prior. At time Burdon was promising to find evidence of those "responsible" for Gar's injuries. Family recommends proceeding with caution. Burdon may be dangerous.

"So what do you make of all this?" I said when I'd finished reading. I had a good idea as to the truth of everything now, but I wanted confirmation.

"Burdon isn't dangerous anymore," Nob said. "Also, it would make more sense as to why Holdsclaw would want him dead."

"But only if Holdsclaw really had done something wrong during the war." I put my boots back on.

Nob nodded.

I was getting tired of travelling back and forth across this cursed city, but it looked like I was going to have to do it again.

X. A Third Visit

"No. You and your thug may *not* go in."

We were back at the guardhouse that led into the Gardens, and my friend Colby was at the podium.

"The matter is urgent," I said.

"I don't care if you were dying of poison and only Lord Holdsclaw had the cure. You're not getting in." Colby waved his hand in a shooing motion. "Lord Holdsclaw told us unequivocally that he should not be bothered – and he named you *specifically*. Now scurry off back to whatever travelling circus you came from before I have the guards throw you out." Next to the door that led through the gatehouse into the grounds the long-haired guard seemed to be giving his club a few practice swings.

"We're going in," I said and started walking past Colby. "If you don't want to get hurt, stand aside."

"Security!" he shouted and the guard came with his club at Nob. At the same time, I felt a tugging at my loose tunic from behind. "You're not going anywhere you little demon!"

In one swift motion I spun around and swung my

arm straight backwards at shoulder height as forcefully as I could. Due to my size, which Colby, ironically, loved reminding me of, my shoulder height lined up almost precisely with the space where his legs came together. The back of my knuckles struck a fleshy part and the grip around my tunic was released. Colby whelped, pig-like, before toppling to the polished stone floor. Just to be a bitch and because I was angry about Lord Holdsclaw lying to us and Lila leaving me, I walked over to where Colby lay and gave him one last swift kick to the throat.

By the time I turned back around, the guard who'd attacked Nob lay moaning on the floor and my partner was playing with his mustache.

"Let's hurry up before more guards come," I said. "We don't want to turn this into a sword fight."

"Let me give you a lift," Nob said, getting down onto one knee.

I hated this, but I wasn't much of a fast runner and we needed to hurry. I hopped on his back and he started running towards Lord Holdsclaw's cottage.

We pushed past the servant who answered the door, despite his protestations.

"Lord Holdsclaw! We need to talk!" I called. I was no longer riding Nob's back.

We found him in the house's library sitting at a desk, drinking from a bottle of wine. He looked markedly less charming than the first time I saw him. He was still just as handsome though.

"Getting the evening festivities started early?" I said.

He took another swig. "You two have a lot of gall, coming here," he said.

"Why do you say that?" I said. "The unfortunate business with your assassin?"

"*My* assassin. I do believe you've gone crazy. How about for lying to me about not going to the summerhouse?"

"Shandra was there, wasn't she?"

"How about for not bringing her back here then?" The bottle was still three quarters full, but judging from his slurred words, I was guessing that there'd been a bottle that preceded this one.

"She didn't want to come here," I said.

"Well, no matter. She's here now. I had some of my servants find her and she arrived a few hours ago."

"Where is she?"

"Upstairs resting. All this business with Gar had quite an impact on her. She'll forget him in time, though. I won't have you bothering her, if that's what you were thinking."

"So you're saying you had nothing to do with that assassin?"

"Of course not! Gar may have been a liar and a scam artist and no good match for my daughter, but that's no reason to start sending assassins around. Are you mad?"

Far at the edge of my periphery vision, I saw Shandra, unmoving, watching our conversation. I made no motion to her; I don't think her father, in his current inebriated state, noticed her. "I admit that it would be rather... extreme to hire an assassin for those reasons. What do you think, Nob?"

"I agree: extreme," he said.

"The man's criminal past undoubtedly caught up to him," Holdsclaw said. "Live by the sword, die by the sword."

"That would make sense," I said.

"Then, let us call these matters to a close. My servant will see you paid. On your way out."

"Yes. Okay then. We will just be leaving," I said. I started to turn away just so I could see the expression on the bastard's face: relief. "One thing I forgot to mention, though."

"What?"

"We learned who the impostor Gar Mallott was."

"He's dead now. It doesn't matter," Holdsclaw said.

"But aren't you curious?" I said.

"Not really. One would-be thief is the same as the next."

"His name was..." I looked to Nob. "Purvis?"

"Torvis... Torvis Burdon," Nob said.

"Yes. That's right, Nob."

"A strange coincidence that Burdon actually *knew* the real Gar Mallott," Nob said.

"More than *knew*. They were the best of friends," I said. "At least until Gar was hurt in the war. Gar was never the same after that. The real Gar, that is." I'd obviously never met the real Gar, but from what I'd briefly observed of the fake one, I suspected they were more than friends. I imagined Burdon sitting at Gar's bedside, feeding his beloved spoon after spoon of thin porridge as Gar looked out vacantly at a world that now meant nothing to him.

"But you know what else I heard, Nob?"

"What?"

"That Torvis blamed his friend's injuries on a traitor. A traitor who profited by supplying the Alliance with provisions and weapons and intelligence during the war and at Xanthas."

"Stop boring me," Lord Holdsclaw said, but I could tell from the look on his face that he wasn't bored.

"Hey, Lord Holdsclaw," I said, "didn't you actually get rich by supplying the Imperial army with provisions during the war?"

"What are you suggesting? Leave me!"

"Wow, that *is* a coincidence," Nob said. "But I'm sure it's just that. A coincidence."

"Probably," I said back to my partner. "But wouldn't it be terrible if, hypothetically, someone *did* have evidence that a certain wealthy merchant was a traitor? Might that be a reason this hypothetical wealthy merchant might send an assassin to kill that someone?"

"I'd definitely send an assassin to kill them," Nob said.

"Get out of my house!" Lord Holdsclaw dropped the bottle and the remaining contents spilled onto the floor. "You know nothing and insinuate everything. All you're doing is annoying me."

Shandra was out of sight now, I noticed, although I wasn't sure when she'd left.

"You're wrong. I do know about some things," I said. "Like the bank records your daughter stole from you that would serve as evidence of what you did. I don't know if Burdon told her why he wanted them, but there's no way he could have gotten them without her help. The one scroll we found at Burdon's house didn't have anything damning on it. My guess is that either Shandra stole the wrong document or else the right one was on Burdon when he died. Either way, I'm sure that the Imperial Bank has duplicate records that would be available if the Grand Councillor's Office wanted to investigate."

"What do you want? Money? How much is this going to cost me?"

I looked at Holdsclaw with all the contempt I could muster. I didn't want money. I wanted Burdon to be alive and that fool assassin too. I wanted Gar to walk again and Lila to come back to me and Shandra to have a chance at happiness. I wanted justice. I was about to say something to this effect but, as always seemed to happen whenever I had a noble-sounding speech at the ready, I was abruptly interrupted – in this case by a crash upstairs. Nothing too loud, more just like a heavy item falling off a shelf. None of the three of us made a sound.

I tried to think how long it had been since I'd last seen Shandra – what was possible in that amount of time? I wasn't sure so instead I just ran toward the staircase.

XI. The Third Body

If she hadn't tied such a skillful noose, if the stool she'd stood on had been just a little shorter, if she'd weighed a stone or two less, Shandra probably would have survived.

It was less than half a minute after the crash that the three of us, along with two of the servants, were upstairs. However, by the looks of things, one second after the crash would have been two seconds too late. Shandra hung from the rafters of her bedroom, her neck tilted at an impossible angle, her eyes wide open but seeing nothing. As opposed to most of the amateurish hangings I'd witnessed (or indeed experienced, but that was another story), Shandra died the clean death of a snapped neck.

Lord Holdsclaw propped the fallen stool back up and stood upon it. "A knife! Get me a knife!" he screamed to the servants who went scurrying. Nob drew his sword and stood on his tiptoes to saw through the rope. The body came down suddenly, but Nob was able to toss his blade aside and catch the corpse before it fell over onto the floor. Nob laid Shandra's body down gently.

"Don't touch her," Holdsclaw said and pushed Nob aside. He looked at her once and then called to the servants who were still fetching a knife in the other room. "Get a healer!" It was clear that any healer's efforts would be in vain, but I kept my mouth shut. He'd figure it out soon enough.

Lord Holdsclaw came down off the stool and pushed Nob aside. He was visibly crying now. "Get away from her! Get out!"

Nob looked at me and I nodded. We headed for the stairs. As we left the house, and the sounds of Lord Holdsclaw's sobbing, behind us, I thought about what to do next. Should I go to the Grand Councillor's Office and tell them of everything we'd learned? That was the proper thing to do, I guessed. Still, we had little direct evidence and what might we hope to accomplish? Seeing the headman's axe fall one more time would do little to fix all the blood that had already been spilled. The war was over. And besides, maybe Lord Holdsclaw had already been punished enough.

---

*Prior to returning to school to pursue his MFA in Fiction, **Cam Rhys Lay** worked for a decade doing online marketing and publishing pretentious (but beautiful) leatherbound books. His fiction has been published or is forthcoming in Eclectica, The Society for Misfit Stories, and No Extra Words. He is currently finishing his first novel. To learn more about Cam and his writing you can visit his website at www.camrhyslay.com.*

The Christmas Cracker

A Ghost Story

Rafe McGregor

"There may be possibilities, too, in the Christmas cracker, if the right people pull it, and if the motto which they find inside has the right message on it."

M.R. James, 1929

I

The internal architecture of No. 10 Flowergate is rather unusual. For one, the ground floor consists of a single large room, apportioned to a reception area, dining-room, and sitting-room-cum-library with the strategic deployment of furniture. For another, the kitchen is on the first floor, although the inconvenience is compensated for by the presence of a water-closet. Both are the result of the idiosyncrasy of a former owner; the conversion of the small drawing-room into a study that of the current owner. The second floor is also out of the ordinary, comprising two bedrooms of ample and equal size, one which overlooks the front of the premises and the other the rear. The domicile is thus perfectly suited to the pleasant cohabitation of two independent gentlemen and it was this consideration amongst others that had prompted me to invite Mr Wilfrid Fletcher to take up residence there. I have recounted the curious circumstances of our meeting elsewhere and I shall only say, by way of introduction, that his health had recovered fully and that he was gainfully employed as the Under-Sheriff of Whitby by the time of our second Christmas together in 1908. Fletcher had suggested that I invite Largo Delapena, the flamboyant American editor of the *Dailygraph*, to join us for Christmas dinner – which was how I came to be opening the door to that very gentleman at eight o'clock *post meridiem*.

"Mr Delapena, do come in out of the snow."

He was a slim man of medium height, with a somewhat ghastly pallor to his flesh that was accentuated by the fact that he was always clad in black from head to foot. His hair was worn rather longer than fashionable, his moustache rather smaller than fashionable, and his clothes harked back to an earlier era, including a top hat, Ascot Tie in the Regency style, and a cape to keep off the snow. Although we had never met, I had seen Delapena many times, usually carousing in the public bar of the Royal Hotel, and I wasn't sure if he was my own age, mid-fifties, or younger but looking older. Both the darkness and abundance of his brown hair also muddied the waters in this regard. The bags under his eyes spoke of lack of sleep, profusion of alcohol, or a combination of the two, and I had indeed never seen him without a drink in his hand.

"Good evening, sir!"

I took his hat, stick, cape, and gloves and then offered my hand. "I cannot recall that we have ever been introduced. My name is Roderick Langham and this is my particular friend, Mr Wilfrid Fletcher."

He shook hands with both of us. "Delighted, delighted. I know Mr Fletcher better as the Under-

Sheriff, but I confess I know very little about you, sir, except that you frequent the Royal Hotel every Wednesday night and are associated with the Literary and Philosophical Society."

"I imagine nothing gets past you in your capacity as editor of the *Dailygraph*, Mr Delapena, but I see that you are also a keen observer of your fellow man."

He waved graciously. "There's no need for formalities, Mr Langham, no need."

"In that case, may I ask your indulgence in sitting down to the dinner table at once. My housekeeper insisted on serving us and I do not want to keep her away from her kith and kin."

"What would you like to drink?" asked Fletcher.

"A glass of gin, with a little sugar and water, if I may."

"May I suggest a sloe gin, in keeping with the season?"

"Very good!"

Fletcher poured the gin for Delapena, a glass of red wine for himself, and a glass of water for me.

I raised my glass to Delapena. "To your very good health."

"My health is always excellent, sir, so allow me to drink to the health of my hosts instead."

We saluted each other and imbibed our beverages. I invited Delapena to sit at the table, took my place next to Fletcher, and rang the bell to let Mrs Knaggs know we were ready.

Delapena glanced quickly about him as he sat. "Three chairs of course, but I wonder where you have stowed the fourth?"

Our small dining table was made for four, but there were only three places set. "You really are a keen observer, aren't you?" I chuckled. "The fourth has been permanently relocated to my study. I find the hard chair assists with my back pain."

"You are a writer, sir, confess it!"

I raised my glass to him. "You have found me out."

"May I ask what you write?" Fletcher began to say something and Delapena caught his gist immediately. "I have no wish to intrude, sir; it is just that as the editor of the only daily paper hereabouts, you have made me feel something of a fool for failing to recognise your name."

I nodded my thanks to Fletcher. "Can you keep a confidence, Delapena?"

"Of course."

"I write the lurid and improbable tales of Sexton Blake."

"Ah, the *other* Baker Street detective. But I *love* a good mystery, how is it that I've not read any of your work?"

"All my writing is anonymous. I find the payment indirectly proportional to the literary merit and I confess I am somewhat ashamed of the money I have made."

"Not at all, not at all! There's nothing like a good mystery to pass the time of day. You must write something for the *Dailygraph*, Langham, you *must*. Name your price, whatever you wish – just don't let any of my staff know it!" I smiled, but did not answer and was relieved when Delapena turned his attention to the laying of the table. "A bon-bon for each of us – delightful! I do love a bon-bon at Christmas, a British tradition of which I wholeheartedly approve."

Fletcher frowned. "Excuse me, Delapena, don't you mean a cracker? I thought a bon-bon was a French cake or confection."

"Of course, of course. I have an antiquarian turn of phrase at times. They used to be called bon-bons."

"And more recently *cosaques*," I added, "Fletcher is too young to remember." Fletcher was sitting to my right so I reached across my torso with my left hand

and offered my cracker to Delapena with my right. When the chain was complete, Fletcher counted down from three and our combined efforts produced three loud *pops* in very quick succession. Each tube contained a sugared almond, a motto, and a paper crown. "I don't wish to be a killjoy," I said, "but perhaps we can forego donning the crowns since there are no children present."

"Seconded, seconded. This almond is delicious! Where did you get these crackers?"

Fletcher had been responsible for the Christmas arrangements. "I had them sent up from Fortnum and Masons."

"Very good! I shall order some myself next year. Will you read your motto first?"

Fletcher unwrapped the piece of paper and read: *"Some say that ever 'gainst that season comes Wherein our Saviour's birth is celebrated, The bird of dawning singeth all night long: And then, they say, no spirit dare stir abroad; The nights are wholesome; then no planets strike, No fairy takes, nor witch hath power to charm, So hallowed and so gracious is the time.* Shakespeare. From *Hamlet*, I think."

"Yes, he describes a holy time when evil is kept without. Shall I be next?" I opened mine. *"By the pricking of my thumbs, Something wicked this way comes. Open, locks, Whoever knocks.* Still Shakespeare, but not quite in the Christmas spirit, I'm afraid. What a strange choice. It is your turn."

Delapena opened his motto and gasped. He recovered quickly, but what little colour he possessed had drained from his face, leaving the flesh a deathly grey. "Mine's very short. *"Now hast thou but one bare hour to live, And then thou must be damn'd perpetually!"*

"Well, that's in very poor taste!" cried Fletcher. "Please accept my apologies. I shall write to Fortnum and Masons and complain. Not just inappropriate, but lazy too. Three quotes from Shakespeare in a single batch."

"I agree," I said, "but that wasn't Shakespeare. It was Marlowe."

Delapena nodded slowly, still shaken. "From *Doctor Faustus*."

II

It was close to ten o'clock when I assisted Mrs Knaggs in removing the remnants of her magnificent pudding and custard along with the crockery and cutlery. I left Fletcher settling Delapena down in front of the fire with a glass of port and a cigar. He had already finished the sloe gin on his own, though he seemed none the worse for it. I had just persuaded Mrs Knaggs that it would quite all right to delay the washing up until the morning or even, heaven forbid, much later, when Fletcher appeared with a couple of empty glasses. Mrs Knaggs wished us both a good night and a merry Christmas and left the kitchen.

As soon as she began her descent, Fletcher leaned forward and whispered to me. It was quite unnecessary, but he was obviously anxious not to offend our guest. "Do you notice the resemblance!"

"To whom?"

"To Edgar Allan Poe, obviously. My God, old chap, it's not just unmistakable, it's uncanny!"

"Perhaps. I believe that Poe has inspired a number of imitators of not only his works, but his appearance and habits. Delapena may be one of them."

"If so, he's done a damned good job of it."

"Don't keep him waiting. I'm going to brew coffee. I assume you don't want any tea just yet?"

Fletcher shook his head and departed.

When I joined them shortly after, they were deep in discussion about the scandal in the Belgian Congo. They were both drinking port and Fletcher was smoking one of his Black Russian cigarettes. I had just sat the coffee tray down on the side table when there was a knock at the door. Delapena started visibly – knocking back his port in an effort to conceal his sudden consternation. "I'll get it," I said, since I was still standing. I had no friends other than Fletcher and his social circle was almost as small so I was curious as to the identity of our interloper.

When I opened the door, no one was there. It was still snowing, although more lightly than before, and Flowergate was covered in a thick, white blanket. A couple was walking down the street, so far away that they were almost out of sight. Perhaps it was someone making mischief, someone who had knocked on the door and then bolted up Cliff Street, but when I looked at the pavement outside the door there were no footprints. I returned to the fire.

"Who was it?" asked Delapena, his visage grim, grey, and lined.

"No one. Well, someone must have knocked, but there was no one there when I answered. You aren't expecting anyone, are you, Delapena?"

"Of course not, what do you take me for!"

"Do excuse me," I replied, "I meant no offence."

"Nevermind, nevermind. My fault entirely. I was just a little startled."

I sat down in my chair, poured myself a cup of coffee, and began packing my pipe.

There were a few seconds of uncomfortable silence, which Fletcher broke. "I say, Delapena, would you mind if I asked you a personal question?"

"Not at all, not at all; help yourself, young sir."

Fletched cleared his throat. "I was wondering if you were by any chance related to Edgar Allan Poe?"

Delapena nearly choked on his port and I had to rescue it while he coughed and spluttered. Fletcher rose to his assistance and offered a handkerchief.

"I am sorry, Delapena, I had no wish to alarm you!"

Delapena coughed again, tears running from the corner of his eyes, and laughed, the sound high in pitch and unsteady in tone. "No, no, you just made me laugh so much I could not control myself. Poe, the poet! Really, Fletcher, what do you take me for – his son?"

Fletcher frowned. "No, you'd have to be his grandson. He died fifty years ago, I think, or perhaps sixty."

Delapena chuckled, more evenly this time, and took charge of his port again. Fletcher refilled his glass and I noticed the bottle was nearly empty. He still showed no signs of intoxication.

"Poe died without any offspring," I said. "I believe he never recovered from the death of his wife and his commercial publishing ventures were entirely unsuccessful. His end was rather tragic, I'm afraid."

Delapena picked up on my point about publishing and commerce and we soon left the topic of Poe behind.

III

The clock struck eleven and Delapena excused himself to perform his ablutions upstairs. As soon as he was gone, Fletcher leaned forward. "I didn't mean to upset him, but I'm sure about the resemblance." He leaped to his feet. "Tell me if you hear him coming back. Where is your Poe?" I had acquired all four volumes of the Ingram edition of *The Works of Edgar Allan Poe* for my modest library. "Here we are, *Volume I – Tales* will suffice. Aha, just as I thought. Look at the frontispiece, the photograph!"

Fletcher was right. The likeness was indeed remarkable and except for the white shirt and light coloured overcoat Poe wore for his sitting, the man represented in the photograph looked very much like our guest. "Do you not think Poe slightly fuller in the face than Delapena?" I asked.

"I do not! Even if he is, the hair, the eyes, the moustache – it's his twin!"

"Or his doppelganger if you have read Poe's 'William Wilson.'"

"Should I show him the photograph?" asked Fletcher.

"No, not after his reaction when you suggested a familial relationship. Also, if I remember correctly, 'William Wilson' does not end well for the protagonist. Poe's stories seldom do." I heard the creak of floorboards above. "Quick, put the book back!"

Fletcher did so, but Delapena returned to silence.

"Don't allow me to interrupt, gentlemen, pray continue with your conversation."

Fletcher gaped for a moment, saw *The Journal of Philosophy, Psychology and Scientific Methods* I had placed in the bookrack, and said: "Darwin. Evolution and all that."

I had to prevent myself from smiling because Fletcher's chain of thought was so transparent. Our clandestine conversation was about Poe. Fletcher's favourite of Poe's tales was "The Murders in the Rue Morgue". The antagonist in that particular story is an Ourang-Outang, which according to Mr Darwin was one of the apes from which human beings have evolved. In his panic to find a topic of conversation, Fletcher's gaze had alighted on my *Journal*. We had recently had a discussion about an article called "The Evolution of Pragmatism" which, as its title suggests, is about pragmatism rather than evolution. With Poe and his ape in mind, however, Fletcher had recalled the title and proceeded directly to Darwin.

The ruse seemed to work and any awkwardness was avoided. Fletcher had just lit Delapena's second cigar with a lucifer when there was another knock at the door.

Delapena's head swivelled so quickly I thought he must do himself an injury.

"My turn," said Fletcher, who was still on his feet. He extinguished the lucifer, dropped it in the ash-receiver, and proceeded to the door.

In order to prevent the escape of all the warm air, I had positioned a Welsh dresser and a pair of bookcases between the dining table and reception area, a strategy that had the added advantage of maintaining the privacy of the library. As soon as he realised this, Delapena ceased craning his neck and turned back to me. "Evolution, huh. That reminds me of your young friend's mention of Poe. What do you make of him – as a writer, that is – from one author to another?"

I could not help but smile this time, the chain of thought coming full circle. "I make no pretensions as an author, Delapena, but I am, I hope, a careful and considerate reader. Mr James Russell Lowell provided an excellent thumb-nail sketch when he..." The door shut and Fletcher joined us. "...Who was it?" I asked.

"I don't know. There was no one there." He seemed rather more disturbed than one would expect.

"You seem to be prone to pranksters, gentlemen, that must be it." Delapena puffed on his cigar, his equanimity apparently restored.

I thought the notion unlikely myself, but did not want to upset him. "Yes, you must be right. Perhaps someone of whom Fletcher has made an enemy in his official capacity." Fletcher raised his eyebrows as he sat down and reached for his drink. I continued before he could contradict me. "Delapena was just asking me my opinion of Poe and I was about to quote Lowell. Do you know that Lowell was a regular visitor here?" I asked Delapena.

"I do, in fact. Only because I took an interest in his poetry, of course," he added hastily. "Did you ever meet him?"

"No, he had been dead several years before I moved here. Are you familiar with any of Lowell's work?" I asked Fletcher.

"I had no idea he was a poet, but I knew of him as the American ambassador, from 1880 or so onwards, I think."

"One of the Fireside Poets of the last century, with Longfellow and a few others. I have several of his volumes. To return to your original question, Delapena, I think it's in *A Fable for Critics* that he writes: *Here comes Poe with his raven, like Barnaby Rudge Three fifths of him genius and two fifths sheer fudge.* I have not read all of Poe's *oeuvre*, but Lowell's rhyme certainly captures my opinion of what I have read."

Delapena smiled and nodded. "Very good, Langham, very good! Three fifths genius and two fifths fudge. Any man should be pleased with such an epitaph."

"And what about you" asked Fletcher, "what do you make of Poe as an author?"

"I think he was lacking in foresight."

"Foresight? How so?"

"He did not, for example, think that his *tales of ratiocination* as he called them would prove more than a passing fad. If they are indeed a fad, they are a fad that has lasted more than six decades and shows no signs of abating. Am I not right, Langham?"

I laughed. "Quite so, but please don't put my

potboilers in the same category as Poe's detective stories. I assure you, they are entirely lacking in merit, literary or otherwise."

"I am sure you are too modest and poor old Poe could have escaped the poverty of his last days had he made more accurate an estimate of the demand for the tale of detection. As it was...hard times, hard times indeed. Yes, *he* fell into despair, but I think he would have been content had he known his legacy would be three fifths genius – *I* would have been."

For the next three quarters of an hour we dissertated on the merits of the various writers of detective stories since Poe.

IV

The clock began striking midnight.

"Is that the time already? I fear I am abusing your hospitality, gentlemen."

"Certainly not, Delapena. Fletcher and I are solitary and serious-minded individuals and it is a rare treat for us to entertain so stimulating a guest. We have no need to rise early, so why not stay a while? I shall attend to the fire, Fletcher will pour you another drink, and you can light another cigar while we are so engaged."

As Fletcher and I rose, he said, "Remind me to attend to the clock, tomorrow."

I opened my watch. "It is keeping good time."

"Yes, but it just struck thirteen."

When we had resumed our places with cigar, cigarette, and pipe alight and port poured for Delapena and Fletcher, the former resumed. "My favourite Poe tale is not in fact one of his tales of ratiocination, but a comedy, a farce even. Have either of you read "Bon-Bon"? I thought not. It is a rewrite of one of his earliest efforts, "The Bargain Lost", and was first published in the *Southern Literary Messenger*. It concerns a pompous French chef and self-proclaimed philosopher by the name of Pierre Bon-Bon. One night while working on one of his expositions, the philosopher is visited by the devil in the form of a tall, lean man wearing green spectacles. He and Bon-Bon begin drinking, with the chef becoming very drunk as the devil regales him with stories of all the different souls he has eaten. The devil then pulls out a signed agreement where, for great mental endowments and a great sum of money, a celebrated luminary has signed his soul over. Bon-Bon is instantly attracted by this bargain and offers his own soul. Luckily for him, the devil is a gentleman and refuses to take advantage of a drunkard. The tale ends with the drunken philosopher-chef collapsing on his floor, his soul safe."

"Forgive me," said Fletcher, "but that does not sound like a very substantial story. With so much to choose from in Poe, I am surprised you value it so. What, may I ask, is the appeal?"

"Oh, it is purely personal. The optimism of the man to think that the devil would not do a deal with a drunkard. As I said, Poe was lacking in foresight. Would you excuse me a moment?"

Delapena rested his cigar on the edge of the ash-receiver and ascended the stairs. His need of the water-closet was not unexpected; he had consumed the better part of the two bottles of port he and Fletcher had shared, in addition to the bottle of sloe gin. As soon as we heard his footsteps overhead, Fletcher leaned forward again.

"What happened when you answered the door?"

"There was no one there. The street was empty."

"Were there any footprints near the door?" I shook my head. "This is all very strange, Langham."

"Fetch that Poe, again, will you. Does it say when he was born?"

Fletcher had the volume open in a trice. "January the nineteenth, 1809."

"I thought so. His centenary is less than four weeks away."

Fletcher returned the volume to its place and resumed his seat. "Why do you ask?"

"I cannot quite say."

We heard Delapena's tread again and when he reappeared, we were discussing the merits of Shakespeare's comedies over his tragedies.

Delapena sat down, drew on his cigar, and had a long draught from the port glass Fletcher had refilled from a new bottle.

There was a hammering at the door – three hard knocks, much louder than before.

Fletcher and I both started in fright. We glanced at one another and then at Delapena, who was strangely unmoved on this occasion. He replaced his empty glass on the side table, his hand perfectly steady, and took a deep breath. "I believe it is my turn, gentlemen."

He smiled, rose, and walked to the door before either of us could protest.

We both stared after him and heard the door open. A few seconds later, I felt a draught of cold air. The clock ticked and the fire crackled, but there was no other noise. Ten seconds passed, then ten more. The room grew chill. Fletcher grasped the arms of his chair.

I stopped him: "I'll go."

Delapena's hat, stick, gloves, and cape were gone and the door was ajar. I opened it fully and looked out. It had stopped snowing. A single pair of footsteps led from our doorstep to the right. I could see two men walking down the hill; one was obviously Delapena, the other was very tall. As they passed beneath the street lamp, the tall man turned to Delapena. I could see his green spectacles in the gaslight. I closed the door and returned to the sanctuary of the sitting-room.

"Well?" asked Fletcher.

"I do not think we shall see Mr Delapena again," I replied.

Rafe McGregor *has published over one hundred and twenty short stories, novellas, magazine articles, journal papers, and review essays. His work includes crime fiction, weird tales, military history, literary criticism, and academic philosophy.*

Mr Kitchell Says Thank You

Charles Wilkinson

"Then he saw a bone sticking out of the cliffs!"

Clayton leans to his left, but Captain Hawbery's blazered back is to him; the conversation is inaudible. Although he's been seated too close to the kitchen door, Clayton shares a view of the North Sea corrugated beneath the morning's sweep of scudding grey sky. Once the Captain has finished whispering at the people who'd occupied the window table before Clayton could reach it, he whips out a notepad and begins to write down their order.

The walls are covered in paintings of ocean-going craft from the eighteenth century to antiquity: barques, schooners, brigs, galleons and triremes. The photo-realism favoured by the artists lends the scenes a static quality; a man of war is suspended on an exquisite, jewel-still sea beneath clouds that never knew a breeze. In the hall, there is a ship in a bottle. Clayton's been waiting for ten minutes for the Captain to take his order, but now his host is walking towards him.

"No kedgeree this morning, Mr Clayton."

"That's all right. I'll have the..."

As he pulls out the menu from under the morning papers, Clayton's aware of the Captain's air of impatience, which appears to be reserved exclusively for him. If he doesn't choose soon, the man will come round and loom behind him, jabbing a tobacco-stained finger suggestively at the scrambled eggs. The Captain's appearance and hygiene are atrocious. His blazer is shiny and various in its shades of blue; the brass buttons absent or unpolished; the white chinos un-ironed. His tie, which is striped and emblazoned with silver rams, is the only comparatively clean item of clothing. Although his long, narrow face is a wrinkled brown, as if from many hours on the bridge, he gives off an odour of grease and garbage. Clayton decides that, in spite of the guest house's nautical theme, the Captain has surely never commanded anything more commodious than a coracle.

"...scrambled egg?"

"Yes, that will do. No, actually... two soft boiled eggs and buttered soldiers. There haven't been any messages for me?"

"Nothing that I am aware of in person. At a moment when we are less busy, I will ask Mrs Hawbery."

The Captain walks back toward the window table, his steps cautious, as though braced for stormy weather. His lank grey hair reaches his collar. As he bends towards the guests, he mutters something that Clayton can't catch. Laughter all round. Then one of the women turns towards Clayton and smiles, gleefully appalled.

The hotel on the cliff top must surely be preferable to the Marine Guest House and Clayton has considered taking his custom there. But he cannot be sure how long it will take him to find Buldatch. His financial reserves will not be conserved by frittering away money on four star accommodation; besides, the private detective has not come cheap. In spite of attempts to give a contrary impression, Clayton is no holiday maker. He has come to collect the elephant.

As she turns off the main road, Mrs Hawbery folds her
umbrella before another gust can turn it inside out.
For fifteen years, Mr Kitchell has lived in the end
house of The Boulevard, which in spite of its name is
not a grand, tree-lined avenue but a steep, unadopted
road, perpetually muddy and potholed. Residents have
made repeated attempts to resurface it economically
with gravel, but every storm washes it downhill to
collect in miserable moraines near the main road
along on the coast. From time to time, the potholes
are patched up with tarmac and other materials, but
no repairs last long. By the end of winter, the road
seems to have been subjected to sustained mortar
attack.

A shimmering blade of water from a previous deluge
breaks into daggers of light and flows downhill.
Buffeted by a cold cross wind, Mrs Hawbery recalls
how she told the Captain that she would not walk up
The Boulevard for anyone but Mr Kitchell. The houses
on either side of her are holiday homes built between
the wars, before the availability of cheap vacations.
Most are occupied all year round, but a few retain the
shabby air of forgotten seaside romance. The stucco on
the end house, which is a bungalow with a spacious
wooden porch, has been freshly painted. Just beyond
the neat front garden and the gate posts surmounted
by stone elephants lies a picket fence that conceals a
railway track. As Mrs Hawbery skirts the last of the
rain-filled potholes, she spots Mr Kitchell standing at
the picture window. He does not wave or acknowledge
her. In spite of this, she rings the bell and enters. By
the time she has taken off her mackintosh and gone
into the front room, Mr Kitchell has moved away from
the window and is standing, his hands clasped behind
his back, next to a fireplace of a baronial magnificence
ill-suited to the proportions of his bungalow.

"Ah, Mrs Hawbery. Thank you for coming on such a foul day. And how is the Captain ?"

"He's not taken to that Mr Clayton of yours. One troublemaker on every ship, that's what he says."

"Really? It's many years since I've had dealings with Clayton."

Although Mrs Hawbery doesn't say so, she can't imagine Mr Kitchell mixing with tweed-suited Mr Clayton, who wears a paisley silk square in the top pocket of his jacket and flashed a gold cufflink when he signed the register in royal blue ink. Mr Kitchell is a clever man. You can tell that from all of the books, but he has an accent she can't quite place: not local but not class either. He's heavily built too. With his broad features, big hands and bat ears, he looks more like a labouring man. Then there's something un-English about him that she can't quite classify. Today she puts it down to the tight black curls of his widow's peak – and his collection of elephants, which she has just begun to dust.

"The Captain was never one for the gentry. He prefers the ordinary folk. The ones that have come across from Stoke-on-Trent. Or the bucket and spade brigade: the families. Not that we get many of them these days."

"Clayton's a retired lecturer who taught at the same provincial university for thirty years. He's not one of the landed gentry – although he wanted to be a Cambridge don."

She's concentrating on the largest of the porcelain African elephants; one prized by Mr Kitchell almost as much as the stone carving in his study. At first, she hadn't wanted to clean for him. Wasn't there more than enough for her to do at Marine House? But trade had been poor and when there was trouble with the bank, it was Mr Kitchell who'd helped out with a loan.

"I've told the Captain, we've got to take what comes

through the door – and like it. But he won't listen. 'I'm not having that bugger in Marine House for another whole week, I can tell you!' That's what he said to me this morning. Right after we'd had two cancellations."

She puts the elephant back on the shelf, positioning it so it's exactly in line with the others. Then she turns round. There's no sign of Mr Kitchell. The carpet's the colour of sand and for moment she wonders how a man of his weight could have moved off without making a mark: not a dent; it's as if the tide has wiped it clean.

When it's time for her to leave, he pads out of his office and hands her an envelope.

"Tell the Captain not to worry about Mr Clayton. He'll be off in a day or two."

She's halfway down The Boulevard when she wonders how Mr Kitchell has heard what she said when he wasn't even in the room. For a second, something's cold and strange in the crosswind and the way the trees shiver high up on the Roman Camp. Then she reminds herself he could have been responding to what she said earlier – or perhaps he was outside in the corridor, listening. She puts her hand in her bag and wonders whether it's worth putting up her umbrella.

Mr Clayton has secured a seat at the window table and is on the point of picking up the breakfast menu when the Captain comes in, a piratical glare in his eyes. He moves broadside before placing two hands like grappling irons on the edge of the table.

"This table is reserved for parties of more than two persons."

"You're telling me I have to move!" says Clayton, mixing outrage with incredulity. "There are no other guests." He waves a hand at the empty tables. "As you can see perfectly well."

"The Mixons, a family of five, will be joining us in this very dining-room shortly. And so I would be obliged, sir, if you would be seated elsewhere."

He hesitates. The Captain is perfectly capable of refusing to serve him. Clayton has arrived by train. Without a car, the alternative is to carry two suitcases up to the hotel on the cliff. "Oh very well," he says, flinging his crumpled napkin on the table. "This is perfectly ridiculous and I shall expect a discount for having been inconvenienced."

"Thank you for your co-operation... sir," says the Captain, coldly civil. He turns away quickly before Clayton remembers to give his order.

The papers have been put out on the side-table along with a few glossy magazines devoted to interior design and country living, but it's the *County Gazette* that catches Clayton's attention: a front page photograph shows a group of smiling Rotarians presenting a silver trophy to a bemused youth. Behind them stands Buldatch in the act of applauding. The caption gives no names except for those of the Club Secretary and the recipient of the prize, but Clayton knows he is not mistaken. Even though his adversary, whose shape is less sharply defined than those about him, is on the periphery of a poorly composed picture shot in bad light, he is indubitably Buldatch. Exuding a mixture of power and amusement, he is simultaneously the most important person present and the only one on the verge of vanishing.

It is a decade since Clayton saw Buldatch and over thirty years since they met at a university in the north of England. From the very first, Clayton had been aware of an antipathy between them. He was on every course that Clayton offered. In seminars, Buldatch would place himself on the seat nearest the window and sit in half smiling, contemptuous silence, until the last five minutes, when he would produce a reference to a writer or an article that Clayton had heard of but not yet read. On other occasions, he would ask the very question that Clayton feared most, one which he had pondered but not yet found an answer to – or even properly understood. Either way, the other students would be left with the impression that Buldatch was far more learned and capable than their tutor. In time, Clayton took to implying that Buldatch was an intellectual magpie, a skimmer of texts with a good memory for names, rather than someone who considered important philosophical problems with profound attention. Although outwardly unperturbed, Buldatch, aware his teacher had never completed a PhD, in spite of having gained a creditable first at Cambridge, began to call him *Dr* Clayton. It was galling to have to correct this as if it were a simple misapprehension.

When the Mixons finally arrive en masse, the Captain takes their order before turning his attention to Clayton.

"So sorry about the delay... sir," he says with some satisfaction. "But I have been informed that the Mixons' taxi is already on its way. I said I was sure you, being such an obliging gentleman, wouldn't mind if they was to be served first."

"I don't suppose you happen to be a member of the Rotary Club?"

For once, the Captain appears first wrong-footed and then pleasantly surprised. "Yes, sir. As it happens, I do have that privilege."

"Then do you know the name of this man and where he lives?" Clayton pushes the paper towards him and points at Buldatch.

"No," replies the Captain, with a shake of the head and recognition in his eyes. "I've never seen him before. He might be a member of a different branch. He doesn't look like a local man to me."

As soon as the Captain turns his attention back to the Mixons, Clayton slides the paper into his briefcase. The information he'd received from a former colleague who'd been holidaying on the coast is correct: Buldatch is living in the village or close by.

When his breakfast arrives both boiled eggs are hard. He decides against sending them back and half an hour later he is showing the front page of the purloined *County Gazette* to the postmaster:

"That'll be Mr Kitchell that you'd be after. He lives right up on The Boulevard – at the very top. I can't remember the name of the place off hand, but you can't miss it: it's the last one before the railway line."

"You couldn't by any chance tell me if he still deals in antiquities?"

"I've not heard it spoken of. Leastways not round here."

In their final year, all students in philosophy at the university where Clayton had taught were asked to submit a dissertation on a topic of their choice. Buldatch selected neo-Platonism, a subject in which Clayton was the department's only authority. At first their meetings were marginally more cordial than expected. Buldatch was an assiduous and alert student. Nevertheless, it was not long before animosity resurfaced. It seemed to Clayton that Buldatch was concerned with the more hermetic aspects of the neo-Platonic tradition at the expense of issues that were still of strictly philosophical interest. But perhaps what disturbed him most was the revelation that Buldatch had applied to pursue post-graduate studies at Clayton's old Cambridge college. Buldatch passing through the Porter's lodge, quibbling over metaphysical questions in its courts, dining in its ancient hall: a prospect that Clayton found unpalatable to the point of nausea. He still loved and visited his college. The thought of Buldatch belittling Clayton's intellect and teaching abilities to people whose good opinion he still valued! And besides, Buldatch was simply not a Cambridge man. At first, Clayton thought the problem was easy enough to fix: he simply awarded Buldatch an upper second instead of a first for his dissertation. When this decision was reversed by the external examiner, it was clear Buldatch would secure the necessary first. Clayton, who'd previously written Buldatch a cautious but not unflattering reference, was forced to use his connections. His allusion in a letter to his pupil's occult interests, combined with a somewhat embroidered account during a private telephone conversation, ensured no offer was forthcoming.

After lunch, Clayton walks up to the Boulevard. The houses have been painted pale yellow, pistachio green or vanilla. Clayton once had relatives who lived on the coast. The cold wind brings the sensation of half forgotten beach holidays: a memory of ice cream vans; the taste of crabs and crayfish; an easterly shining on the shingle.

The end house is set back very slightly from the others. As Clayton walks past the stone elephants and up the path, a train clatters along the track on the other side of the fence. Now that he is almost on the threshold of his adversary's home, unease replaces hatred and indignation. Perhaps he should pack his bags and go to the station.

After Buldatch left the university, there were reports that in place of post-graduate academic pursuits he had joined the epigones of some self-appointed Parisian magus, a man of unknown ancestry with an interest in marrying eastern mysticism to esoteric occidental knowledge. Clayton reminds himself of the origin of the word "gibberish" and rings the bell.

Silence. He walks towards the picture window. On the shelves are rows of elephants in varying sizes and materials. But he cannot see his carving, the artifact his family believed could be the oldest representation of such a creature in mankind's history, predating cave paintings. No Buldatch. Possibly it is just as well. If they are to meet, it will be on neutral ground. Now all he has to do is put his invitation through the letter box.

When he was a boy, the Captain saw them: the men crawling out of the soft cliffs after a storm. They were made of red earth, fragments of rocks, filaments thousand of years old, an odd bone. They didn't last long. The wind blew them away, leaving nothing that wasn't osseous. Sometimes a jawbone would be left stranded in the wrack. The best part of them would be indistinguishable from sand. Later on when he moved to the fishing port up the coast, learnt his trade, the tide's rhythms, the places where the fish sleep, he took a trawler out and forgot about the dead men: how they'd accompanied his walks on the days after a part of the coastal path had crumbled, uncovering ammonites, the fossils of animals not seen since records began. It was only when the fishing failed and he moved back home that he thought of them late at night, when he'd a tumbler in hand, and wondered what kind of child he must have been. Then Kitchell came to the village: he saw the men and more.

A guest hands his key in at reception; the post arrives: only one letter that looks as if it might be important. The Captain opens the envelope and read the instructions. If there's one person he doesn't want to break bread with, it's Clayton. But at least there'll be a decent meal to be had along with a bottle of Bordeaux for his trouble, both buckshee. Seems Mr

Kitchell isn't keen to meet Clayton on licensed premises, but feels he owes him a meal – although not his company until later. The Captain's to explain.

"I'm off out tomorrow evening," the Captain says to his wife, who's laying the tables in the dining room.

"Really? Where?"

"The Highclere Hotel. Mr Kitchell's business."

"Very nice for some, I'm sure."

This Clayton and Mr Kitchell: they didn't seem the type of men to have been mates, although there was no telling. Perhaps the friendship soured. Anyway it was none of his business. If there was one person he was happy to run errands for it was Kitchell. There was nothing the man wouldn't do for the village. He'd bought the Highclere after it'd failed, put money into Marine House and not asked for a penny back. Even the new goalposts for the pub team – they'd been bought by him. And who was it who'd had the wits to see a beast's bone sticking out of the soft cliffs? Mr Kitchell. And he'd bought all sorts in: palaeontologists, archaeologists, men from the council, tourists; it had done wonders for trade at the time.

The Captain is about to retreat to his office behind the reception desk when the doorbell rings and Clayton comes through the front door. The man's wearing a trilby and an overcoat of brown tweed. If his brogues hadn't been a tad too shiny for a racing gentleman, you'd say he'd been watching his prize horse taking a canter in the paddock.

"Ah, Mr Clayton… I was wondering whether you might have happened to see the copy of the *County Gazette*. The side table in the dining-room would be where it's kept."

"I don't think so. What do you want yesterday's paper for?

"The *County Gazette* is a weekly publication, sir. Since 1923."

"Well, I've no idea where it is."

"The point being... sir... that the periodical is one what's reserved for the use for all our guests, not just perusal by one person."

"Quite, quite. My key please."

"Certainly, sir. Only if you happens to run across the *Gazette* somewhere amongst your possessions... like I said, the side table is where it belongs."

It's already dark when Clayton begins the walk up the hill to the Highclere Hotel. To his left is the old coast path that he's been told ends in a wire fence a few feet from the cliff's edge and the sheer drop to the sea. The gulls and terns have vanished into the still night. The only sounds are the scratch of the tide on invisible shingle, the crunch of his footsteps on the gravel road. He has been told that once years before there was a golf course, but erosion has long ago taken the first tee along with the memories of drives and putts.

The hotel's floodlit: a drama of black and white; stacked chimneys – mock Elizabethan; brick balustrades and stairs leading to porticos and enormous oak doors. The building's strangely shaped and has the trick of being larger than it looks from below. There are no lights on. Every entrance has the appearance of having been shut for a century. Following the wall round reveals projecting bays, mullioned magnificence, even a flint tower, squat in comparison to the neighbouring gables, and without any obvious means of access. With a shock, Clayton realises that not a single vehicle is parked on the drive. Then at last a double door at ground level: a glimpse of varnished wood and the gleam of brass; the steady shine of light, strawberry blonde to copper-red – the colours of welcome.

Clayton steps through into a vast entrance hall: high

ceilinged with Gothic arches and faux-medieval tracery; a floor of black and white tiles, and at the far end a wooden reception desk running the length of a wall honeycombed with cubbyholes. To his right is a bar separated from the lobby by decorative wrought ironwork. As he steps through, he sees there is only one table on which rests a vase filled with white flowers. There are no seats, but a stone settle has been carved into wall; for a second, he's reminded of a side-chapel dedicated to some vanished saint, whose name alone survives.

"May I help you, sir?"

Having seen the metal grille, he'd thought the bar not only shut but unmanned. Now he notices a figure clothed in black, waiting – as if to hear a confession.

"I assume you're not serving."

"On the contrary, I am happy to be of assistance, Mr Clayton. You are expected. Go through to the dining room, which you will find beyond the ante-chamber at the end of the corridor."

"I'm meeting a Mr Kitchell. Perhaps you know him?

"Wait in the ante-chamber."

Clayton glances at this watch. "I'm early. I'll stay here for the moment. A gin and tonic – with ice and a slice of lime."

"Which we will bring to you in the dining-room," says the man, before retreating through a curtain covering an arched doorway.

The absence of cars outside has prepared Clayton for a lack of guests. Yet it's only as he crosses the entrance hall, hearing each footstep, even the echoes individual, that he becomes aware of the strength of the silence he is disturbing. The corridor is unexpectedly constricted, its panelling dark and oppressive; so it's a relief to emerge into a spacious ante-chamber, windowless but lit by chandeliers. There is no furniture, but an enormous map of the county occupies most of one wall. As Clayton moves towards it, he sees the coastline cannot be contemporary: there are promontories submerged long ago; estuaries and inlets since redrawn. There are no villages, towns or cities – even roads are absent; only the details of an ancient physical geography are marked: rivers, lakes, marshes, forests, the higher ground in the north.

"Please come through, sir."

A waiter suddenly at his shoulder. Clayton's unclear if it's the man behind the bar.

"The hotel isn't at all busy. Is that usual at this month of the year?"

"We are always fully booked, sir. The residents prefer to remain in their rooms."

"Really? Why?"

"They are elderly. Some are susceptible to the slightest draught; others wish to conserve the energy for tomorrow's event."

"And what would that be?"

But already they are walking across a deep burgundy carpet. Every table in the dining-room has been laid but only one is occupied, by a man looking away from them. A sweet trolley is to the side of him, from which he is ladling mounds of a mauve and yellow dessert. The dark stained walls are lined with the mounted heads of beasts, only some of which Clayton can identify. The one over the great stone fireplace is surely a spotted hyena.

"Captain Hawbery. Your guest has arrived."

The Captain does not stand up, but turns slowly towards them. The bottom half of his face is smeared with sherry trifle.

"So you're here. I've made a start, as you can tell. But I'm not as far ahead as it looks. I likes to work my way backwards through the menu."

"This is a mistake," says Clayton, turning to the

waiter. "As I've already told you, I'm here to meet a man called Kitchell."

"This table is reserved for Mr Kitchell's guests, sir. The drink that you ordered will be with you shortly."

Before Clayton can reply the waiter moves away soundlessly across the carpet. For a second, it seems the man is an attribute of the building's function, brought into existence to provide a service. The Captain has lined up seven profiteroles on his plate and is swaddling them in clotted cream.

"What are you doing here?" Clayton asks.

"Mr Kitchell appreciates the kind offer, but he is unavailable until tomorrow lunchtime. Says this meal is on him, being as it's his hotel."

"Really? The hospitality trade. I wouldn't have thought that was his line," says Clayton, sitting down with some reluctance. "So we're to lunch here. Is that the arrangement?"

"No. Particular in his diet, is Mr Kitchell."

"You're very well informed for someone who professes not to know him."

But the Captain's turned to welcome the arrival of a trolley sailing towards them with a shipment of sides of rare roast beef, pink lamb, boiled hams, chicken breasts, a piglet complete with Cox's apple, pyramids of potatoes, great silver gravy boats and ten kinds of vegetable.

"The Highclere carvery. None better!"

"So where am I to meet him?"

Unwillingly, the Captain switches his gaze to Clayton.

"The steps at the cliff's edge lead down to the Hotel's private beach. He will meet you there at noon. Now are you after a starter or will join me on these mains here? Mr Kitchell says to build up your strength now, as it's quite a climb down. And oh... you're in for a rare treat tomorrow. It will be his way of saying 'thank you'; that's what he told me to tell you!"

The truth is here on the coast. Mr Kitchell repeats the words as he stands outside his home. He is filling in two of the potholes in the road, which threaten to expand and absorb their neighbours, creating something close to a water feature. He straightens his back and rests for a moment on his spade. The Boulevard frames a wedge of sea and the smudged white horizon. A trawler appears immovable, as if fixed on its strip of green water. Above the houses on the right lie the cliffs: the wind-flung gulls are powdery white specks, visible against the reddish-brown rocks, before fading into a pale blue sky. On its headland, the Highclere Hotel seems to have crept closer to the edge, ready to outpace the rate of erosion and crash into the sea in clouds of masonry. As an investment, its value dwindles but it will outlast him, at least in his guise of Mr Kitchell.

At twelve o'clock, he is to meet his former tutor for the first time in a decade. He smiles as he recalls their previous encounter, an occasion on which Clayton failed to recognise him. Then it was wise to remain incognito, as it was necessary to relieve his tutor of an item possessed in law but not by any moral title. So of course, he hadn't been able to thank Clayton at the time. For in spite of the maelstrom of ignorance and malice that did duty for the man's teaching method, a debt was owed. Of course, he had been aware from his first term that the ordinary language philosophy that Clayton practised, which permitted him to patronise neo-Platonism as a historical curiosity, was of no importance; it was examining a grain of sand without seeing the beach, let alone what was on it. What's more Clayton might look at his grain from every possible angle, without ever, to paraphrase Blake, seeing a world in it. By cheating him of Cambridge, Clayton had set him on the road to true understanding: the occult as the sacred in the ordinary; how to practise "being" in the illusions of time and the persistence of place. Perhaps what was needed at noon was a demonstration; yes, that would be a way to show his gratitude.

Now the Captain's wife is present, weaving her way past the potholes.

"Everything that was here," says Mr Kitchell, rubbing his hands gleefully, "is still here!"

"Well, that's a relief, I'm sure," Mrs Hawbery replies.

"But it's not a question of having the time to look into it, but a way of looking into time."

"Now you've lost me, Mr Kitchell. I think I'll just get on, if you don't mind. The Captain thanks you for the meal by the way – although he was not so keen on the company."

Mr Kitchell opens the front door and follows her inside. Once the dusting of the elephants begins, he retreats to his back room. Here there is only one carving, which is kept on his desk. How many thousands of years had passed since the craftsman held his simple tools of stone? For this is surely one of the earliest representations of such a creature. Is it a tribute object of some forgotten tribe? A way of exercising authority over a part of the sentient world? Cradling it in his hand is to recover what can be experienced but never fully explained. But for Kitchell it contains a vestige of totemic power: a way of coming closer to the first acts of creation. To use it, is to move in the shadow of God's hand.

Clayton's sleep has had the texture of a primordial place: waking from night-walks through woodlands, moist and superabundant with vegetation, he heard the wind tearing through the night, only for him to sink into a sea shared with starfish and crabs.

He was smaller than a newt; his limbs formed like those of a fish. Now he climbs up the road towards the Highclere Hotel. Clouds are the tatters of last night's storm above the foam-shred sea. He is glad of the tweed coat he bought in Cambridge. Though his nocturnal visions fade, he imagines the layered ground beneath him, home to ammonites and micro-fauna, the bones of extinct birds and lizards.

For a minute, the hotel on the cliff vanishes. He wonders if he has taken a wrong turning, only for it to reappear as he rounds a corner, its black and white facade and high gables stark against a scurrying sky. It would have been better to meet Buldatch in the bar. A poor night has made Clayton less inclined to climb down to the beach. Perhaps he should crane over the cliff and tell his pupil to come to him.

It's ten years since Clayton took the elephant to the auction house for valuation. Afterwards, he'd upbraided himself for failing to recognise the bearded, clammy-handed connoisseur, who'd persuaded him to leave the carving there for valuation. Rumours of his former pupil's death by drowning had reached him, and even though the man's accent had aroused unpleasant associations, he had not identified him. Only later, after the disappearance of the elephant along with the putative expert, did he understand how he had been deceived. Now it's evident Buldatch has risen again as Mr Kitchell.

Once again, the gravel-crunch under his feet; no cars on the drive; the great doors firmly shut – and yet there is movement in the windows on the upper storeys: almost human shapes, the colour of clay, darker than terra cotta. He cannot see their features; the angle of the heads suggests they are gazing down.

Then as he stops to look at them more closely, they withdraw into the darkness of the room behind or escape into the folds of the curtains.

He's at the edge of the cliff. The wooden steps are almost vertical. He puts his foot on the first rung and stares down. There is no sign of Buldatch: just the yellow-grey sand, darker near the strandline; a scattering of shingle, the rock pools where children once searched for crabs; the tide's arrangement of wrack. He calls out. No reply.

Perhaps the man is waiting further along the shore. Evidently there is no choice but to make the descent. He clambers down past the many-coloured layers, the geological ages captured in waves and stripes; the mineral glitter gives way to chalk. He stands on shingle then sand. As he stares up, they are gathering on the cliff tops: the Hotel's grey and rusty ghosts, sightless yet observant. Then a squall blows away the head of the largest one. A shiver runs through the others as they struggle to hold their shape.

It's low tide. Groynes guide his eyes over the length of the bay; the furthest is half submerged, a jagged line like an alligator's back. The sand nearest to the sea is slick in the glare of noon.

"Kitchell... Buldatch?"

The wind picks up, reconfiguring the seaweed, stirring the dry sand in the cliff's shadow. Halfway along the beach is a wooden hut, once used to sell ice-cream. It's just possible Kitchell will be waiting for him in there. As picks his way round the rock pools and mounds of seaweed, he wishes he had chosen sturdier shoes. Then on the periphery of his vision, he spots a disturbance in the cliff face. He turns, but is too late to see clearly; only an after-image of a dust-red man, wriggling into the rock.

The shutters on the hut have been pulled down. The

wood has been bleached to silver and appears almost friable.

"Buldatch!" Two insignificant syllables tossed into the strengthening gusts. The sea is choppier, freaked with foam. Is it possible that Buldatch has arrived after him and is even now descending the steps? As Clayton swings round, he's at once aware of the hotel, perched on the very edge of the cliff. His fresh viewpoint has rearranged its walls so it now seems less wide at the base than on its rooftops. It's leaning over the precipice and peering down at the beach. He's too far away to spot anyone at the windows. Is it the curtains that are fluttering like eyelids? He is witnessing something that is architecturally impossible or a strange trick of perspective. As he stumbles on, the hotel appears to withdraw slightly, not wishing to tempt gravity.

Then a rock to the right of him cracks open, followed by a cascade of tiny stones, a trickle of minute pebbles. A fracture in the crag exposes a shape like a horn. Soon a second point appears. Something bellows behind the cliff face – a sound as old as the ice age. The horns splinter chalk and quartz – and turn to tusks. Slowly it emerges, shrugging its shaggy limbs, creating a cave where it slumbered. Twice the size of an elephant, it rolls out its mighty trunk and stretches, shaking off the dormant centuries. With a roar, the mammoth storms towards him, crossing the not-now to each new minute, replacing its footmarks on the sand.

Charles Wilkinson's publications include The Pain Tree and Other Stories (London Magazine Editions) and Ag & Au (Flarestack), a pamphlet of his poems. His stories have appeared in Best Short Stories 1990 (Heinemann), Best English Short Stories 2 (W.W.

Norton, USA), Unthology (Unthank Books), Best British Short Stories 2015 (Salt), London Magazine, Under the Radar, Prole, Able Muse Review (USA), Ninth Letter (USA), The Sea in Birmingham (TSFG) and in genre magazines/anthologies such as Supernatural Tales, Horror Without Victims (Megazanthus Press), Rustblind and Silverbright (Eibonvale Press), Phantom Drift, Bourbon Penn, Shadows & Tall Trees, Prole, Nightscript and Best Weird Fiction 2015 (Undertow Books, Canada). He lives in Powys, Wales, where he is heavily outnumbered by members of the ovine community. A Twist in the Eye, his collection of strange tales and weird fiction, is now out from Egaeus Press, including stories that first appeared here in Theaker's Quarterly Fiction.

The Cutting Room

Chuck Von Nordheim

This happens to Peter Felix almost at the end.

Peter turns his back on the Master and the Adirondack-sized doses of euthanasia it doles out in the murk below. He grabs Willow's wrist; she tries to resist, but years spent toting the one-thirty-eight pound burden of *The Oxford English Dictionary* has supplied him with the prowess of a WWE wrestler. With her in hand, Peter kicks and shoves against the press of half-dressed and naked undergrads queued up for the Master's lethal blessing, forcing her back toward the university subbasement.

What he has observed immediately becomes complete to him, becomes inaccessible. He has always lived like this, disengaged from his own life.

In accordance with his dreams, Peter Felix has located the hidden passage behind the hinged health promotion poster in the student union, the one that shows a double-chinned Henry VIII devouring Photoshopped pizza above a legend that *just say no to the third slice*. He has descended the spiral stairs that unfurl into lower darkness after he pushes down on the antique fire alarm. He has entered a cavernous space lit by luminescent constellations of fungi anchored in the cracked walls, a forgotten subbasement beneath the tunnels that provide access to campus classrooms during inclement weather. In this secret space, in this amber light, Peter Felix has seen dozens huddled.

When Peter Felix passed a new judgment, the act became something that had always been so. His altered position – on the superiority of Franklin numbers over Johnson numbers or the pre-eminence of Stealing Sheep over Arcade Fire – became a historical fact. He passed the judgment below on the day he started his teaching assistantship while he walked through the food court where the Henry VIII poster hung.

Bits of undergrad conversation – pop culture references to redshirts and Mary Sues, arguments crippled by *post hoc* fallacies and either/or reductions – bored into Peter's ear. The complete and utter lack of intellectual attainment evidenced by this random sample saddened him. It struck Peter that they seemed more like movie extras who exist to do a single act – wait for a train, swing a sword – than true college students. He decided it would count as an act of mercy to fail the majority of the freshmen who took his sections of first-year composition. How could minds obsessed with the plot gyrations of *Game of Thrones* and other such twaddle survive in an environment that demanded critical engagement with the poems of Emily Dickenson and other sophisticated texts? In the long run, they would appreciate an early notice of their insufficiency.

Surely Peter had driven to the student union, but it seemed to him, no doubt due to his excitement over his summons from the Master, as if he had teleported from his bedroom to the university campus. Why should he have kept track of such mundane details as what route he took from his graffiti-adorned apartment complex or where he had parked his twenty-eight-year-old Camry LE liftback when a supernatural mentor had signalled its willingness to free him from all of the impediments that blocked his progress? Peter had affixed Stealing Sheep decals to his rear bumper, good-enough guides for locating his car if he still required ground transportation after the Master rearranged his destiny.

Stray remnants from REM sleep, the equivalent of counted yarrow stalks for Peter Felix:

- The Master will tower above mere humans. Peter will see legs and the bottom of a torso and the ends of arms, but height and distance will obscure its face.
- The Master will own iron-hard skin. Peter will hear echoes reverberate when he slaps his hand against it.
- The Master will hold balls of light in each hand. The balls will thrum like well-maintained engines. Their colours will shift from blue to red to white. Their beauty will capture Peter's gaze. He will regain his nerve, heart calmed by the sublime nature of the humming lights.

Willow told Peter this somewhere between the time the Henry VII poster swung back and the subbasement swung open. To Peter, though, it seemed like she had spoken the words long ago:

"Film Studies teaches the cruelty of editing." Willow said. "A savvy director shoots the same shot with a different lens, writes two scenes that make the same point. A smart director wants options – the fight scene in wide angle versus soft focus, a voiceover by the goofy sidekick versus the sultry siren – when she shapes the story in postproduction." She wound a strand of green hair around her finger. "From a director's point of view, it's an expected part of process for terabytes of footage and for multitudes of characters not to make the final cut." She crooked her knuckle, making the green strand taut. "A big-ass deity like the Master would have to do the same, wouldn't it? For the sake of the bigger story, delete superfluous characters and plot arcs that didn't pan out. Of course, no actor likes ending up on the cutting room floor."

Peter Felix passed this judgment less than a day ago, but already it seems a fact that has always been.

One trait shared by the dozens huddled in the secret subbasement shocked Peter. Their seemingly consistent student status did not bother him; he assumed the Master summoned other categories of initiates to different secret locales. Their uniform state of dress, or rather undress, temporarily caught him off guard – terrycloth robes, plaid flannel lounge pants, oversized school sweaters, and naked goose-pimpled skin – their condition made sense, though, if the Master had called them all in the midst of a dream; looking down, Peter saw he too had driven to campus in his bedclothes. But why would the Master have picked so many recruits on academic probation? Many gathered in the subbasement were the same clueless individuals that Peter and his fellow teaching assistants had ridiculed for their inability to write an intelligible thesis statement, let alone a sentence where the predicate commented logically on the subject, once the doors that guarded their suite of cubicles were locked. Gazing at the huddled dozens murmuring in the glow of the mushroom light, he could only deem them a worthless clot of losers.

Peter speculated the general fecklessness of the balance of the crowd supplied the reason for his summoning. Those pathetic excuses for students would need someone to lead them, and Peter's three semesters of manning the teacher's podium had endowed him with full knowledge of classroom leadership. For the greater glory of the Master, he would serve as their captain.

He has always existed apart from his past, separated from its pain; these events happened two weeks ago, but for Peter they may as well have taken place in the nineteenth century.

The clack of a doorknob latch has sounded. Startled, Peter has bolted down the white-stuccoed corridor that connects the offices of the English department's tenured faculty. An L-shaped bend in the hallway has offered him a haven; he must see how his sweet professor reacts to his gift. For minutes, Peter has watched her examine the valentine with a baffled expression; attuned to the interpretation of her every gesture by his prolonged desire, he reads the shapes her lips make. Silently, she has formed the words *Peter who?*

Before Peter learned her true name, Willow spoke to him. He watched her push through the naked and half-dressed mob – Goth style copying Rossetti, well-nourished body mimicking Rubens – and greet him with open arms. For Peter, the dialogue played out like an old song on YouTube – distorted, crackled – even though he spoke his piece in it.

"I wondered when you'd show up, Mister Felix," the

green-haired girl said. "I pegged you as a definite invite to this party given your absolute inability to make yourself part of anyone else's life." Crimson lips smiled. "Of course, it takes a zero to know a zero. Let me introduce myself." Black lacquer polish glistened. "I'm Willow Swan, better known as Award Acceptance Girl, the biggest loser in the Film Studies program."

Peter stared at the offered hand. "You seem mistaken, Willow," he said. "I'm not like you. Not in the least. I'm a grad student."

"Really?" she said. "You're not the sad jackass of a TA who achieved the lowest score ever on Rate My Professor? You're not the pathetic dork in khaki pants and a tweed coat who forced his classes to watch weekly PowerPoint presentations on his unrequited love for his thesis advisor? You're not the pretentious jerk in a polka-dot bowtie who took off points on quizzes if you couldn't remember what poem he glued on his valentine to his sweet professor? It's funny. Your face exactly matches the one on all the dartboards within fifteen miles of campus."

"I'll tell you all you need to know about me." Peter thrust his thumb at his chest. "I'm the one the Master picked to whip you undergraduate misfits into shape. I'm the one in charge."

For Peter Felix, key scenes of his intellectual unfolding had seemed always in attendance in his consciousness; he might have related the effect to a specific variety of mental imprinting if psychology had meant anything to him. The memory of the winter afternoon when his hatred had blossomed for J.K. Rowling and her fellow traffickers in literary soma for kids, for example, had remained forever present, the incident spurred by the chance inclusion of poem 112 by Emily Dickinson in his middle school reader – R.W. Franklin's numbering being the only system a true scholar referenced. Peter had never questioned why none of these continually available moments linked to revelations about arithmetic or epiphanies about history or the comprehension of love.

Some certainties from the roil of Peter Felix's dreams:

- He will obey when the Master calls. He will do this out of reverence, not because of the promises the Master has made.
- He will carry out any task the Master assigns to him. He will do this out of love, not because his superior abilities ensure he will hold a position of high rank.
- He will trust the Master to set him free. He will do this out of faith, not because the sundering of his socioeconomic chains will permit Professor Green to love him.

As soon as words were said, they seemed to drift to the distant past. Even in the moment when Peter staked his claim for command, this occurred.

"So," Willow said, "You plan on taking charge of this operation."

"The Master picked me for that duty," Peter said. "It summoned me here for that reason."

"We all received the same call," she said, "directions to the secret stairs behind the poster plus some wish-fulfilment fantasies. I think you got some of your info scrambled."

"For all you know, I could be the Master," he said. "I could be incognito checking out the situation."

"You're wearing Pokémon pyjamas," she said.

"They make an ironic statement about current culture."

"Dude, the Master wouldn't wear Pokémon PJs."

Peter judged Willow six months before the Master summoned him, though once decided upon it seemed to him that he had always held the opinion he rendered. Peter did not know her name then and a chance crossing of paths supplied the occasion for his determination.

In the campus tunnels in route to one of his sections of first-year composition, Peter heard a rattle of metal and the flap of plastic. He looked back and saw two running figures: a stick-thin man with a beard to his waist in a turquoise elbow-patch sweater trailed by a green-haired woman in black fishnet stockings and a loose-fitting black caped coat with a suit bag draped over her right shoulder. The suit bag did the flapping and rattling. Peter identified the pair on sight based on the scuttlebutt out of the film studies department: the Full Frame Kid, the undergrad director whose short feature on tattoo discrimination got slotted at three major festivals, and Award Acceptance Girl, the crazed groupie who appointed herself Kid's official formalwear wrangler. Girl shouted for Kid to wait, but the bearded man ran faster; he rolled his eyes back so far that Peter could only see their whites. Pressing against the tunnel wall as they charged past, Peter assessed their relationship the most dysfunctional one he had ever witnessed and deemed Award Acceptance Girl as the saddest of all women.

Peter Felix avoids the physical, privileges the intellectual. Yet, he wades eagerly into the fray when the situation suggests the possibility of brutal action.

An undergrad in hunter green, shaved head tattooed with Kanji symbols for victory and honour, stampedes through the subbasement. Peter notes these aspects about the onrushing man: kohl-rimmed eyes, a sullen sneer, a white twenty-four on a team jersey used for a nightshirt. The apparent sports fan launches himself headfirst at Peter's chest. On the ground, Peter considers the observed traits and behaviour against people he has met; he identifies his assailant: Austin Stark, a chronically underprepared freshman from one of his Fall 2013 sections of first-year composition. Peter picks himself up. He readies himself for the next attack, cocking forearms made brawny by hefting briefcases weighted down with insipid student essays.

Since none of the women Peter had slept with resembled Professor Amy Green, he had discounted their joy at his disproportionate gifts. Disappointed and saddened by these intimacies, he had blamed his inability to reconstruct in so much as a single case a chain of events before or after the bedroom on the instability caused by the getting-to-know-you bottle of pinot noir. Why should he have worried about the absence of names and phone numbers when he had no desire to see any of these women again? Suppression had seemed the better course of action; he had lived in fear that his sweet professor would learn of his depravities.

To Peter Felix, this conversation seemed to have occurred in a far-off time, even though it happened not long before the end.

Willow used the span of her arms to put distance between Peter and Austin. "Tell me why you two can't play nice," she said. "We're all for the same thing. That should give us reason enough to treat each other with kindness."

"The son of bitch cost me my scholarship." Austin rubbed his forehead. "I got thrown off the team before the season started because he gave me a zero out of a hundred on my literacy essay."

"You didn't follow instructions," Peter said. "I asked for a reflection on a transformative experience with the written word which incorporated the grammar guidelines from the handouts. Instead, you delivered an anthology of misplaced modifiers and pronoun case errors allegedly related to baseball."

"Spoken by a dickweed who knows nothing about sports," Austin said. "Reading a team takes more analysis than reading a poem."

"I saved you from future embarrassment," Peter said. "The business world has no room for rejects who can't write a sentence."

"You need to find a way to forgive each other and you need to do it right now," Willow said. "The Master wrote the script. You two can't blame each other for the crap parts it gave you to play."

Behind Peter Felix's closed eyes, storms of reveries:

- Freshmen will line up for autographs after his workshops on logical fallacies, presenting PowerPoint printouts for a swipe of his quill pen. The students will insist Peter dispensed more insight than Neil deGrasse Tyson or Michio Kaku did during their campus stops.
- In one year, five of his students will win a Rhodes Scholarship; each submits a personal statement that began as a dull literacy biography but which

will blaze into brilliance due to Peter's advice on stance and audience.
- These displays of pedagogic prowess will melt the heart of his sweet professor. Amy will stop denying her feelings. She will reject the teaching assistant/tenured faculty protocols.

In the subbasement, Peter Felix changed his mind about Willow – perhaps moved by the mood the mushroom light induced – and once he did, it seemed as if he had never held another opinion.

The amber light from the walls conjured the magic of the moon and candles; it blurred the desperate lines on her brow, blunted the grossness of a jutting belly and dimpled thighs that demanded the concealment of a loose coat. In this setting, these items of her Gothic ensemble charmed him: her crimson lips, the skulls that decorated the elastic of her panties, the skeletal hands that framed the cups of her black satin bra. Peter decided this is a woman he could love if he ever stopped loving Professor Green.

Willow told Peter this somewhere between the time he pushed down on the antique fire alarm and first time he saw the Master in the yellow-lit murk. To Peter, though, it seemed like the words came from some old text – *Beowulf* or Saint Bede – something half-remembered and barely understood:

"A character doesn't exist if the major players in the plot arc don't respond to what he does," Willow said. "Your case stands as an example, Mr Felix. Does the object of your affection ever respond to anything you do?" She flipped open her robe. "Maybe in a chick flick your nerd moves would earn your sweet professor's unconditional love. But in other genres, psycho moves like those would motivate phone calls to the cops." She adjusts the elastic of her panties. "She finds your valentine and forgets about it. You send her weekly PowerPoint updates with bar charts that graph the upward trend of your adoration and she ignores them. No restraining order, no sexual harassment charges, no reaction – which means you don't really exist."

These events have happened but minutes ago, but already they seem infinitely distant, perfected and put away.

Peter has inhaled Willow's lavender scent, a sensory input absent from his dreams; the odour mingles with the wafts of dank rot from the cracked walls and the stink of unwashed bodies that rise from the surrounding crowd, transmuting the overripe air into a perfume imbued with intimacy and comfort. He has stepped into the aura of her impassioned physicality – the raised eyebrows, the pointed fingers, the thrust out hips that punctuate every assertion – each tic and gesture demanding a re-evaluation of his romantic attitudes.

In his dreams, promises for the future:

- Peter will kneel by a titanic toe, a boulder-sized distal phalanx of a mountain-sized presence. He will swallow his fear. He will remind himself of what his dreams have promised. He will wait for the Master to bestow its blessing.
- The Master will lower its arm. The air will thrum with energy. The colour of the ball held in its lake-sized palm will shift from blue to red to white.
- The ball of shifting light will graze Peter's neck –

perhaps it will leave some mark, an indication of favour. Freedom will follow. All things out of joint will reset.

At the end of every semester, and at Thanksgiving and spring break and Martin Luther King Jr. Day, Peter had sped north in his Camry. Each trip, he had loaded his iPod with new releases from Stealing Sheep and the Staves, and a *Moby Dick* audiobook. He had left campus with the intent of seeing his family, but the details of what had happened after he crossed I-70 eluded him; it seemed he went and came back with nothing but his longing for Professor Green to fill the gap between departure and return. Even the final status of Captain Ahab and Ishmael remained hidden to him. Peter had ignored these gaps and all the other blanks in his life like any extra or walk-on does; he had waited for his moment in the spotlight, the chance to become his sweet professor's leading man.

For most his life, Peter tamps down his yearning for brutal violence, resists its promise of complete connection. Then Willow takes notice of him.

The meaning of the words she says blur for Peter the instant they pass her crimson lips – temporal disconnection weakened the signal and seeded it with static – but the emphatic jiggle of her body makes an argument that overcame all of his objections. Why should he stay emotionally bound to Professor Green when she failed to take notice of him? The purple tassels of Willow's robe tickle the back of Peter's hand. Did he not deserve the warm haven of another's embrace? His palm slides down ripe flesh that curves toward the skull-emblazoned elastic. But before Peter

Felix steals his kiss, a blunt force slams into his groin and he sinks, retching, to his knees.

In his dreams, images of the future:

- He will brush back raven hair from the white cheeks of Professor Amy Green. In their rented cabin, the heat of cracking pine logs will heat their naked flesh. The body of his sweet professor will shudder after hours of tracing her curves, of eliciting wafts of her salty scent, of thrusting to his full length. Done, her blue eyes will glow with complete love.
- Amy will adjust the Windsor knot on his tie in their hotel room. She will carry his laptop in the elevator and rub his bunched shoulder muscles. In the conference room, his sweet professor will fit the network cable into the USB port. She will test his Logitech Wireless Presenter R400 with its built-in laser pointer. She will lead the ovation his explication of the dimensional metaphors in poem 598 arouses.
- He and Amy will walk on a red-brick concourse beside a brown river. Between them, their golden-haired daughter will chatter about the differences between ducks and swans. They will grasp the little Petra's arms. They will swing her up and back, to and fro. Their little girl's laughter will echo through the park while twilight shadows gather.

Willow told Peter this after she kicked him in the balls and before she joined him in line for the Master. As soon as she said, it seemed something that had always been so. As soon as she said, Peter knew he loved her and always had.

"First," Willow said, "I will answer any other psycho bullshit with extreme pain; we're both in the reject pile and that means, unlike the world upstairs, I pay attention. Second, the reason I approached is that you are the only invitee who exceeds my laughing-stock status. I do men with beards, not baby-faced boys. Third, do you not grasp that we are both risqué gags tagged for a particular character's plot arc? I'm the big girl who's small in one place, a perfect fit for a hipster with a micro-penis. You're the awkward twerp who turns out to be well-hung under his bowtie, a hilarious find for a fellatio-addicted PhD. Should the Master delete such lame jokes from its text? Damn straight. Should these two anatomical misfits hook up? Hell no. Fourth, I forgive you. I know how much you hurt. I've chased a love that refused to see me too. So, can't you please try to be cool in the time that's left?"

Peter Felix has experienced these events in the last minute.

One of the lichen-encrusted walls of the subbasement has slid back, revealing a ledge abutting a mist-shrouded space. Far above, a belt of careening yellow flecks has lit the murky expanse beyond the ledge where the Appalachian-high legs of the Master flex and its Ozark-long arms swing. Without a sound, the waiting students have queued up in a line that Peter assumes leads down to its boulder-sized toes; the crowd in front of him and Willow prevents a clear view.

Peter has reached the ledge. From this vantage, he has confirmed the line of students goes down to the Master; other lines of suppliants – all naked or in nightclothes – traverse the murk. Two files of pilgrims have knelt near the Master. A giant arm has swung. The air has thrummed. Shifting colours have dazzled.

Peter has watched each kneeling pilgrim puff into a wisp of yellow flecks.

Peter Felix has slowed his pace so he can keep watching. The ball of force lodged in the Master's palm has turned kneeling rank after kneeling rank into wisps. The Master has selected no favourites, has conferred no blessings.

For once, nothing blocks Peter's access to the emotions vested in that moment. He rages at the Master's broken promises, his stupidity, and the insipid design of the role allotted to him.

Peter had cut the pink construction paper into the shape of a heart while sitting at a beige particleboard desk in the corner of his apartment living room. He had swiped a glue stick across a round of lace and a square of Southward Specialty Parchment Copper; the bond paper had held an elegant, quill-scrawled copy of "To His Coy Mistress" by Andrew Marvell. He had failed to deem odd the under-the-sofa discovery of a box of art supplies he had previously no need for; the surfacing of a hitherto unknown talent for calligraphy had not troubled him in the least. Peter Felix had signed the valentine, embellishing the t and x with twisting vines of fleur-de-lys, and then had marched into the cold morning mist of mid-February with it tucked under his arm.

Peter Felix connects to the world only in moments of intense action – surging muscles, churning lungs. He hates this facet of himself, keeps it leashed like a dangerous animal. Near the end this beastly aspect keeps escaping Peter's cage. This cut of his story starts with Peter fleeing the Master with Willow in his grip. This happens next:

Peter reaches the ramped causeway that leads to the overlook; Willow, penned in a side headlock, still resists but he forces her steps with an occasional squeeze on her jugular. He finds the going easier; the line for the Master has thinned. But will the subbasement wall remain open after the last pyjama-garbed student leaves? Peter increases his pace. A voice yells overhead. He looks up. A green shape hurtles from the ledge. Peter discerns a white number twenty-four in the moments before impact. Then he feels nothing but the smack of rib-shattering momentum.

This conversation happened right before the end. To Peter Felix, it seemed as distant as all the others in his life when it began.

"There's nothing for you back on campus even if the stairs are still there." Austin swiped away the flow from a gouged brow. "That professor of yours can't see you. This girl here can't love you." Austin reached out a hand topped by ripped nails. "I'm saving you from a bad future like you saved me, Mister Felix. The Master offers the real deal, dude. You know that, right?"

For first time, words resonate for Peter in the moment they are said. He groans as Austin pulls him to his feet, the pain from cracked ribs and battered kneecaps lance through him. Peter looks into Austin's kind eyes. He spits out a tooth and then nods his head in concurrence.

"I wanted someone to love me," Peter says. "I wanted to matter." Tears stream down his face and mixes with the blood from his cuts and abrasions. "Why can't I have just that? Why is that too much? It's not fair. It's not."

A gentle arm draws him near. A lush body takes him into her embrace.

"You're right," Willow says. "It's not."

At the end, hopes with eyes wide open:

- He will have tasted a liquor never brewed, at least not for him; he will have known the attention of other humans who share his situation, will have known the sanctuary of friendship.
- He will have taught Willow and Austin the lyrics for "Rearrange". He will have argued for the song's adoption as their requiem and will have explained why anyone with two working ears ranks Stealing Sheep the best band ever.
- He will have let go his dreams about Professor Green. He will have said goodbye to the image of their golden-haired daughter.
- Holding the hands of his friends, he will have knelt before the Master; he will have welcomed the blessings – the possibility for the misshapen to gain new forms, the chance for losers to win in a new game – the Teton-sized titan conferred.

Chuck Von Nordheim *lives in northeastern Los Angeles country at the geo-biological point where chapparal merges into pure desert. Currently, he poses as an MFA fiction candidate at CSU San Bernardino on Tuesdays and Thursdays. The rest of the week, he scours Mojave Desert garage sales and antique shops for Highway 66 memorabilia that he can sell on eBay to pay his tuition. His other magreal/surreal works have appeared in Three-Lobed Burning Eye, Ealain, Twisted Tongue, and Daily Science Fiction.*

Gliese and the Walking Man

Howard Watts

"You've had a difficult few days? *You?*" I could see my great grandson was a little taken aback by my directness and somewhat abrupt delivery. I'm usually relaxed when he comes over to visit us – it's my age, I tend to take things easy now – stress still kills. But this time, no, I couldn't relax. My wife could see that in my eyes, and she returned to the kitchen without saying a word after we exchanged subtle smiles. I guess she knew what was coming.

"It was hard work," he said, slumping into the chair opposite me at the dinner table.

I thought about it again for a short while before deciding to tell him – he probably wouldn't believe me, but there's evidence out there, if he looked hard enough.

"Let me tell you about my toughest few days – and then you can decide if yours were really that difficult. Fair?"

He looked up and nodded. "Fair."

---

1. Orbit

It was just another normal Monday morning to begin with really. Following a small repair detail outside, I sat data monitoring aboard my one-man mid-orbit sat.

PLANET: GLIESE (ZARMINA)
CATERGORY: EXO PLANET/SUPER EARTH

PARENT STAR: GLIESE
CONSTELLATION: LIBRA/RGW

R ASC: 15H 19M 26S
DEC: -07 43' 20
APP MAG: 10.56 TO 10.58
DIS: 20.37LY (6.26 PARSEC)
SPEC TYPE: M3V
MASS: 0.31 SOLAR MASS
RADIUS: 0.29 SOLAR RADIUS
TEMP: 3480+48K
METALLICITY: {FE/H}
-0.33=0.12
AGE: 7-11GYR

ORBITAL ELEMENTS:
SEMI-MAJOR AXIS: 0.13AU
ECCENTRICITY: 0
ORBITAL PERIOD: 32 DAYS
MEAN ANOMALY: 271+48
SEMI-AMPLITUDE: 1.29+0.19

PHYSICAL CHARACTERISTICS:
MINIMUM MASS: (M SIN 2.2 EARTH M
TEMPERATURE: 242K (-31C;-24F)
TO 261K (-12C;10F)

DISCOVERY INFORMATION:
DIS DATE: SEPTEMBER 29, 2010
DISCOVERER: STEVEN S. VOGT
METHOD: RADIAL VELOCITY
SITE: KECK OBSERVATORY, HAWAII
DIS STATUS: CONFIRMED

There were all kinds of traffic – all types of formats, buzzing around for me to monitor, thread and archive if needed. This was just two years following the successful introduction of axial rotation to our adopted planet, eradicating forever her tidal lock, and much of the information I concentrated on consisted of statistical recordings of her internal and external behaviour following this marvellous feat. Data stringers pulsed between sats collecting and delivering encrypted hard data, while my automated equipment – for this shift, anyhow – filtered through the galactic background chatter, looking for a placed theme or signal embedded amid all the junk, hidden for an intelligence to pick it up, to then pass on any string that might have a soul to it, a personality trait worthy of human interpretation. 'Puters still can't be relied upon for picking up such info, even now, not the really complex stuff the coders predict we should receive from something out there, one day. Although as *you* know, we're still waiting.

I sat peering out of the small circular porthole looking down to the surface of Gliese, just watching the cloud formations and weather fronts, picking out a few notes on my acoustic guitar to pass the time of a well-deserved break. It was a beautiful sight below, undisturbed, serene, very similar to old Earth some 20 light years back, albeit as it was some four or so centuries ago. White and grey clouds stretched across the continents and oceans, a storm front moved in over the northern hemisphere as the poles slept in white. It was peaceful, beautifully peaceful.

Then it happened, so damn quickly. They appeared out of nowhere, too small to be detected by the conventional equipment of my day, until they formed up into a swarm, eating their way through all the mid-orbit sats and stations. They said later it was a cloud of robotic / autonomic something or others – tech-eaters someone called them. My proximity alarm sounded as soon as they took shape, so I fired up the thrusters, going manual to try to avoid their course, but they turned quickly like a preying shark toward my little sat as it moved aside. They began eating their way through my sat before I knew what was happening, so I suited up as the engines groaned, struggled and died, and I jumped the locks. The eaters devoured everything behind me so quickly, storing it, replicating themselves with the material they'd gorged upon to move swiftly on.

---

2. Resignation

I found myself floating slowly head over heels in space, my breathing low and laboured. I didn't know it at the time, but I was in shock. I watched helplessly as they moved to their next target, a manned ocean monitoring station some twenty thousand metres away – I knew the family that worked there. It took these alien parasites perhaps ten minutes to wipe out all of the remaining mid and low-orbit sats, then they turned upon the high orbit stations – Home One – bloody great station that was, the docked supply rigs, the three deep space telescopes, Seager Harbour and the arc of twenty ore processing stations that received material from the asteroid miners – can't remember all those stations' names now, it's so long ago. But I do remember many of the people that worked with me on those old boats, still remember some of their faces. Most of them were around my age, early to mid 20s, some a little older – a few vets from the decades Gliese 581g was first settled, back in the 80s. The eaters weren't interested in us it seemed, just our tech and raw materials, the metal, alloys, polymers, glass, whatever. They devoured the lot, leaving the crews naked to space, probably aware they'd never survive. Horrible way to die, having everything eaten away from you like those little fish that eat dead skin from your feet. The eaters exposed everyone to the harsh reality of our old enemy the vacuum – just as they were born my friends and colleagues died, in their thousands. I saw them.

I was lucky, perhaps too small to be significant, as I'd jumped my locks. I righted myself with a suit thruster and watched as the swarm moved away, turning their attention toward Home One. A handful of tiny vessels tried to escape, but the swarm grew, reaching out in the silence to intercept every single one. Then Home One imploded, perhaps a self-destruct to take a few of those alien bastards with it, we still don't know, even today. But I didn't have time to be an idle spectator to this horror, as I realised I was being pulled slowly towards Gliese's upper atmosphere and my death.

It's a damned strange feeling, knowing you're very soon going to die, that there's absolutely nothing you can do to change that fact, that nothing's gonna save you. I was resigned to my fate. I knew without having to check that my suit only had a three-quarter charge, so there was no way the built in thrusters could propel me out of Gliese's gravitational pull – even if they could, there was nowhere to go, as no safe haven remained. Besides, I'd not tanked up on oxygen since my last eva earlier that morning, and was looking at enough air for fifteen or so minutes – hardly enough time for a rescue ship to reach me from a ground station. I remember thinking, what would kill me first, lack of oxygen, or would I have enough to still be breathing as I burnt up in Gliese's atmosphere, plummeting planetside? I closed my eyes and let myself drift.

3. Descent

I thrusted 180 degrees to face Gliese, my adopted home of just a few years, and smiled as I realised how gorgeous it was (far more so than Epsilon Eridani, that old halfway stopover between Earth and Gliese) while I was pulled inexorably toward it. Slowly my peripheral vision was filled by this giant world.

As my eyes wandered across its surface, an object to the left and beneath my position distracted me, a silver edged something, tumbling, glinting again and again as it slowly headed toward oblivion. I watched it closely, realising its fate would predict my own, and with morbid curiosity, I waited, recording its location and rate of descent, to see how long it would survive before burning up, as this would give me an indication of how long until my own excruciating demise would begin and how long it would take. I zoomed in with the suit's eyes, reading off the information, discovering it was a chunk of heat shielding – possibly from Home One or a supply ship – and measurements indicated it was around the size and shape of a standard airlock door. It was too far below for the eaters to pursue, I guessed, perhaps too dangerous for them at such a low altitude, or even insignificant – maybe they'd bitten off more than they could chew, or the shielding's composite left a bad taste in their mouths.

God only knows where the idea came from, but I found myself thrusting toward it, refusing to allow fate to carry me to my death.

I was resolute; I would *not* die that day.

My thruster fire caught the eater's attention and the swarm turned toward me, part of it separating, giving chase. I accelerated, diving headfirst, eventually impacting the piece of shielding, climbing over it as it spun, magging to its inside, halting its rotation with a short burst, letting the exterior absorb the heat as we plummeted. I switched info streams and the suit provided me with telemetry data from a land based tower, the hud giving me all the figures and graphical representations of relative positions I needed as I swiped across screens, and it was then I saw my potential saviours. There were three ore processing downstations on the surface of Gliese back then. All three projected gravity tunnels into the upper atmosphere which ore was deposited into by the automated low orbit haulers. The ore then descended at a controlled rate, to be processed by the unmanned downstations. A crazy idea seized me. If I could glide through each gravity tunnel in turn, their decreased gravitational fields would slow my descent and *perhaps* I could softland, as long as the shielding would hold out, and as long as I was careful and calculated exactly the right amount of thrust needed for that final burst before the suit's juice totally ran out.

I turned on my back and watched the swarm advancing upon me, so I made my initial course correction and increased my rate of descent, heading for the first tunnel. The shielding began to glow from the heat, its edges curling, flaking off in tiny plumes of molten alloy. My suit's hud – powered by embedded dual processors back then – began feeding telemetry data to me as fast as it could, but the processors began to labour, arguing over their conclusions as they double-checked each other's results. They weren't built for this kind of analysis, as the speed of my descent fed them too much data too quickly, and as they struggled to complete a calculation, the data altered, rendering their results inaccurate. There was all this mad audible electronic chatter between the two processors and I knew I had to rely on instinct for the most part to hit the first tunnel with the correct trajectory.

I struck the gravity tunnel with a whack, choosing not to thrust back a little before hitting its field. That was a mistake, and the impact of all those gravitons upon us broke my suit's maglock on the shield, so I reached out and maglocked again with my palms, then kneepads and boots, clinging on for dear life, checking the projected timings for the next burst to take me into the second tunnel.

The swarm were aware their prey was escaping, and they reached out with tendrils, long spindly fingers with glowing tips, constantly eroded by the heat of freefall, continually replaced by their multitudes. A tip finally touched the shielding next to me and instantly it separated into its components before swiftly withdrawing. I watched as the other tendrils retreated, molten sparks of white gold against the blackness above. What they left behind with me were like ants I guess – spiders – but with small eyeless heads and abdomens with six legs, and no thorax, overall around the size of my hand. It was difficult to tell as we shook against the friction. I remember thinking how beautifully engineered and coloured they were, as half a dozen of them walked around the shielding beside me, just a few centimetres away. They looked

confused, bumping into each other, perhaps communicating with each other, waiting for instructions? Then they all lined up together and walked in unison to the edge of the shielding. Thankfully the stupid little bastards began eating through the shield's edge, perhaps a more valuable material to them than that of my suit, and their heads were instantly vaporized as they exposed themselves to the friction, limbs flailing about in confusion before I kicked them off the shield with my boot. Salvation!

I hit the second tunnel with 17% power remaining, and was still too high to discard the shielding, with the final tunnel some two hundred clicks distant. Then I cleared the upper atmosphere and began to believe my crazy survival plan could actually work. Gradually the blackness of space fell behind me, and colours filled my peripheral vision. Below to the left and right I could see clouds, snow-capped mountains and blue lakes peering between them. It was a fantastically beautiful sight. I hit thrust once more, 8% remaining as I headed towards that glowing final tunnel. As my bad luck would have it, it was in use, thousands upon thousands of tonnes of raw material crammed into the field. I had no choice; I had to traverse its entire diameter – measuring a quarter click, perhaps double that at the angle I entered it – to provide me with enough deceleration to survive. I picked my spot, entering faster than I'd have liked, weaving between giant rocks and boulders, and just when I thought I'd made it clear, the shield clipped a rock, and we were separated for good. Perhaps this was a blessing. Now free of the shield it was just me and my suit. I pulled my legs up to my chest, folding my arms across my knees, keeping my head down, letting the field carry me toward the processor's maw. I couldn't stay in the tunnel, I had to save enough thrust to exit it just above its rim – as close to the ground as possible, either that or I'd be chewed up by the downstation's processing jaws. I stayed in that tunnel as long as I could, then thrust out, leaving the last burst of power timed by intuition to help break my fall as the suit's processor arguments became feverish in my ears, until suddenly their voices rose in harmonious agreement – we were, *I was*, gonna make it.

I don't remember the impact as such, I remember tumbling down a hillside, my body bouncing off of rocks, dust and shale all around – perhaps I'd fallen down an entire mountain, I don't know, as that final terrible impact rendered me unconscious.

---

4. Red Sunrise

I was awoken to darkness, apparently by a group nanite charge, a jolt to wake my sleeping heart. My heart beat sporadically at first, uneven, unsure, a broken rhythm of near death, struggling to find the consistency of life. As I teetered on the precipice between this life and the next, my mind swam against the tide of many drugs towards the distant shore of lucidness. It was if I was trapped in a dream, hallucinating all kinds of disturbing images. Had the eaters landed planetside, ravaged Gliese, perhaps having developed a use for and therefore a taste for the constituents of what makes us human?

It seemed to be an age before I had the strength to open my eyes, to move even in the slightest, as my suit had administered meds and painkillers, but as my injuries were so grave – beyond what was the accepted norm for the suit's programming (such as a seal from a micro meteor impact) – my prescription was an almost fatal overdose. I lay there, waiting in the darkness, as my body took what it needed and violently rejected the rest. My nanites were in the final stages of doing what they could for my broken legs, and arm, my dislocated shoulder, knitting and sealing the bones, repairing torn ligaments and muscles, stemming blood loss, releasing nutrients, sealing wounds. They too were now as exhausted as myself, and as I opened my eyes to the suit's hud, the information there flickered then finally faded, drained of charge. My heart regained its natural rhythm and at last I sat up slowly, discarding the helmet to look around. I was in a ravine, and the crawl perhaps an hour or so later to open ground was so painful it was unreal, despite the painkillers.

I felt so lost without any information easily available at my fingertips or a blink instruction, naked against the reality of my predicament without even the basic tech at hand. You realise how much you rely upon these little devices when without them, how you take them for granted to inform you of such essential info, even down to the moods of friends and family, simplistically indicated on screen by a tiny iconic representation of a human expression. You wanna know what the weather's doing? Look out the window. You wanna know how someone feels? Ask them. Just a couple of things I learnt and which I still maintain today. However, at this stage all I needed was a compass and its four indicators. I reached the summit to lie there in the cold, waiting for sunrise, my mind thinking, "Four, four, I need the four, the four points of the compass to steer my way home."

When the sunrise finally arrived it was majestic, the giant red revealing a vast rocky plain stretching before me, with the spires of the city, Gliesia, in the far distance catching the sunlight of that early morning. The colour of the sun retreated behind the atmosphere, thus dulling it, softening it to a palatable orange. It was beautiful. Relief swept over me. The city, the population remained, hinted amid the haze before me. I stood shakily, admiring the spectacle, realising I was perhaps the only survivor of the eater's ghastly heavenly banquet. I waited for the sun to rise higher then headed carefully down the loose shale slope to the plain waiting below, and the long walk to follow.

---

5. Pilgrimage

Saying all this, to be honest it was difficult to decide what to do at first. Should I remain where I stood upon the edge of the plain, in the expectation my controlled freefall had somehow been detected from a surface station? What would you have done? I wondered if perhaps a rescue vehicle was on its way, but then I estimated Gliesia was just a couple of days' walk, and if I stayed put without food or water and rescue wasn't on its way, I'd eventually become too weak to make that journey, and ultimately die in the attempt. Instinct told me to keep moving, as the landscape this side of the city was essentially barren, explored only by the odd automated private rover, despite the time mankind had lived here.

It was almost like a pilgrimage, that long journey from east to west across the surface of this planet, a pilgrimage to the rest of my life I finally decided, and it was going to be a *long* walk. I began, slowly at first, then found my rhythm – evenly measured, kicking up dust and dirt, heading for that far-off city with the sunlight bathing my face. My thoughts were mixed: elation at having survived; horror, remembering the recent demise of so many friends and colleagues, my helplessness as I watched. Would the eaters pose a threat to the inhabitants of our young world as my hallucinations had suggested? Or, were they simply automated miners like our deep range bots, intending simply to harvest, unknowing or unaware, uncaring of the life forms they had condemned to perish in space. There was a distinct possibility they were designed by an intelligence to prevent detection of their homeworld, their actions that day simply a calculated display of power and ultimately prevention. For them, far more effective than entering into a discourse with a race they had no intention of accommodating. Neighbours still erect high fences and allow their boundary hedges to grow taller, even on Gliese. I continued on across the plain, keeping my face toward the sun, picking up my pace as best I could. After half a day I found a small shallow pool of water, hiding in the shade of a rocky outcropping. The water tasted foul but it was needed, and I used it mostly to refresh my face. Then I sat for a while beside that pool, both of us enjoying the shade. I turned my back to the sun to look at those three giant ore processing stations some forty clicks distant.

Balthazar, Caspar and Melchior, halleluiah my three saviours! I nodded to them my thanks in turn, then started walking once more.

---

6. Hope

The landscape was barren way back then, long before the other settlements grew from the rock, before the graphane hyperloops connected the entire planet and its cities. Amid the haze I was sure I could see a flat area of ground, perhaps a roadway leading to the city? This gave me hope amid my fatigue, but then I noticed beyond that to the north the clouds hung heavy in the sky, close to the ground. I knew what was coming – a storm. The weather front I'd seen from orbit had developed, matured as Gliese continued to adapt to the new seasons mankind had coaxed into existence. Back then these fledgling storms, akin to teenage tantrums they used to say, were very unpredictable, so I had no idea what was headed my way. As I continued on I noticed a patch of colour ahead, and as I came nearer, I could see it was a tiny flower, lonely amid the dust. I stopped and bent down to examine it more closely. It was beautiful against the starkness of the dusty ground, delicate purple and yellow petals, with seemingly fine leaves, light green with darker spots near their edges – I remember it distinctly. As the wind rose it swayed and slowly its petals closed upon themselves almost with a shiver, its head bowing slowly as if respecting the coming storm it knew it couldn't survive against. The plant then retreated beneath the surface, vanished as if it had never existed. I wondered if there were more of these delicate flowers hiding beneath the surface, or if this was the last of its kind. I stood and looked back to the north and shielded my eyes as the dust storm approached. Then began to dig, copying the flower's retreat, but my fingertips soon found bedrock. I moved on, digging again, but there wasn't enough depth for me to take shelter as the flower had. I couldn't just stand and wait for the storm to pass, so I continued walking on as best I could, shielding my nose and mouth with my right forearm, my left hand cupped over my eyes as the storm buffeted me.

After what seemed like several hours, my feet found a metallic bar protruding from the ground. I crouched down. My hope was rewarded, as I'd found the edge of the piezoelectric roadway leading to Gliesia – I know, they don't make them anymore. I walked along the edge of the road until the storm dissipated, hoping I was heading in the right direction. The piezoelectric system recharged my suit a little as I walked, the nanites patching it up and I wished I'd held onto the helmet.

7. Running for the Gate

The storm passed and upon the roadway leading to Gliesia, my pace quickened as I saw figures shouting and waving me forward from the towers either side of the city gate. I was elated, the city and its safety, its food and clean water – a cold beer, they'd seen me! Human companionship – and ultimately my family waiting on the city's opposite side, possibly unaware I was alive, all that and more was just two hundred metres distant. Perhaps my freefall *had* been detected, and I was expected. Then I realised with some confusion the gate guards were pointing *behind* me, not *at* me. I turned, the road behind me shimmered in the sunlight, changing, gathering – but no, not the road itself, but rather what was upon the road and around its edges. These small scurrying shapes rapidly formed up upon each other, creating a huge bizarre metallic shape, scared with disfiguring burns and melted black welts. It ambled slowly toward me, jaws snapping at the wind with a horrid measured repeating snap as it reared up, a rasping growl emanating from its maw as it realised its prey was almost within reach. Its movement was like that of a wounded animal, ungainly but nonetheless faster than myself, advancing. As I stood there motionless, transfixed by it, I'm sure I detected an expression across what was its face, an expression of both hatred and elation, perhaps almost a sneer. It staggered towards me, correcting itself with every third step lest it collapse. It was all too obvious this aberration was the remains of the second swarm, and somehow it had survived its own freefall to give chase. Perhaps it had learnt its spindly fingers were useless against the atmosphere, and formed its remaining counterparts into a sphere – the favourite shape of the cosmos. This way some would survive at the core if it rotated rapidly upon descent, sheltered until landfall, its outer layers peeled away by the atmosphere like a huge alien onion, sacrificed for the greater good of those layers protected beneath. I turned and ran.

Running beneath Gliese's gravity is not easy, well, wasn't back then – it was almost like running through shallow water, no, more like running through a dream, or in this case, a nightmare. No matter how hard I pushed my legs forward I couldn't gain speed, as the anger behind me gained ground. I turned as I heard the snapping of its jaws become louder, diving to the roadway as its maw snapped at the air where my head had been moments before. I rolled off the road and over in the dust several times, the shouts from the gate louder and far more urgent. Adopting a gait like that of a sprinter, bent at the waist, head forward, toes pushing against the dusty roadway I gained speed, keeping my eyes fixed upon the gate as it crawled open. A burst of energy erupted beside me, sending shards of sparks and roadway high into the air – another then another, as the guards found their range with their weapons – or rather miners' pulse mortars, used as weapons. Beyond the gate I could see the city's lights, the people, some gathering to watch the commotion. Two guards ran forward either side of me, one of them shouting, *"Down!"* and as I dived across the threshold they obliterated the eater with point blank bursts from their mortars. I turned to see lifeless fragments bouncing upon the road just short of the gate, silver, blue and gold debris that was gathered up by a small group of security guys while others tried to force the crowd back, telling them to disperse.

You know, I was never told anything or even questioned in any great detail about this incident, and you won't find much, if any, info about it in the history files. Okay, it's true this all took place *nearly* a hundred years ago, but it's also a sad truth that unpopular events such as this are easily forgotten if not retold regularly, while other less historically significant proceedings are favoured by whomever records our history files. No one's comfortable with their inability to answer questions – especially historians and politicians – and I had many that day.

---

8. Gliesia

I pushed through the crowd that had gathered at the gate to see what the fuss was about as a blimp crawled across the sky above, casting its shadow over the scene. When free of the masses I instantly became just another inhabitant – and I was content with that at last as I hurried into the streets and anonymity.

The eastern district, the city's founding two mile square area, displayed its heredity proudly, its old Earth origins. The two great eastern powers that had combined their resources and, more importantly, determination to reach Gliese had ensured so. Colour was thankfully important now as much as authenticity. These two powers knew the old cities, as much theirs as well as their many western counterparts, were guilty of having fallen into a monochromatic trap over the centuries of development, a trap of cultural conveniences that favoured the counterfeit and dismissed the authentic. Where once cast grey blocks formed mighty flat roofed accommodation towers, broken up by dull white framed glass, where corporate edifices, tall and defiant, simply reflected the grey buildings around them, here, grey could only be seen high up, represented as a storm cloud's reflection upon the glass. The many dull hues of mock stone, a limited palate controlled by numbered tones, had been wiped clean, here mass-produced plastic no longer betrayed its illegitimacy with an identically repeated wooden grain, as real wood once more became favoured, seasoned, carved, sawn, varnished and polished to display its beauty. No more the painted veins of imaginary granite, no more the textured sandstone lies, or cast fascias representing walls of fake red bricks and render. Gone were the resin columns and capping stones, plastic trees and bushes. Cobblestones were now as dissimilar from each other as snowflakes. I remember someone saying when I was around your age, perhaps in my early teens, all you really need to get by are two 4D printers. If one of their components craps out, just print off a replacement for it with the other. But the founders of Gliese ignored such trappings, for back then, if you wanted to walk on mankind's third adopted home, you learnt, you worked and you lived, you took part in mankind's valued community. They borrowed from an ancient speech; spoken over half a millennia ago, spoken where naturally formed bowls of dust dominated the landscape – just a small phrase to bolster their rules. "For all mankind."

I walked on beneath the towers where the self-sustaining coloured lights burned, illuminating my fellow Gliesians and their contentment. I headed westward, for the most part ignored, my dusty appearance matching that of many a quarryman or stonemason. There was a vibrancy you could feel amid the streets – and I was surprised how beautifully unordered they were for the most part. I'd expected geometric lines, but no, alleyways narrowed and curved gracefully here, encouraging the population to be closer to each other, to face one another as they went about their daily tasks, to become one. Squares suddenly appeared from behind rows of trees where people gathered to talk, to eat and drink, to listen to music and their children's laughter. I found myself suddenly weary, stopping at a bar situated on a corner opposite the Wakefield Theatre.

---

9. Colliding Apart

My DNA was still on file. This relieved me more than you can imagine, as it proved I'd not been declared dead and my identity removed from the data base; that, and the fact I was in credit and could afford food and a drink. I washed up as best I could before sitting at the bar, a curved piece of polished ebony with a brass footrest beneath which my boots thankfully received. I was alone, with just the footsteps upon the wooden floor clicking away as the barkeep topped up a row of glasses from the washer. He gave me a surprised glance before returning to his business. I guess it was a little early for a drink, but I figured I deserved it. As I sipped the ale, the place became busier, people filtering in from the streets, some in silence, others talking in low voices. I glanced at the clock behind the bar – it was essentially lunchtime, and my thoughts returned to my little sat – the journey so far, that near miss at the gate playing over in my head. I couldn't control myself and wept silently as I remembered what I'd witnessed – more from relief than anything else I finally decided, as I tried to stop. Steadying myself, regaining my composure, I forced my shoulders to relax and ordered food. As I watched the bar fill up and I listened to the chatter grow, I found myself saying good afternoon to a woman who had taken the stool to my left. She ordered sushi and lemon tea, unfolding a napkin and placing it delicately across her lap. Before I knew it we were chatting, small talk I guess, nervous release – although I do remember saying to her, "Aliens ate my guitar," at some stage – which afforded me a slowly raised eyebrow. You know,

it's funny how sometimes bars can do that to people,
allow them to relax and open up to complete strangers.
Some say it's the alcohol, but I'm sure that's not always
the case, it certainly wasn't on this occasion – it's more
to do with the surroundings, the relaxed atmosphere.
Okay, it can't be found in every bar, but this one was
abundant with communication. I retold my story as
she nibbled the sushi and sipped from her cup,
cradling it delicately with her long fingers. I watched
her expressions as the steam rose from the cup,
wondering if she believed me, if at all she was
listening – I was innocuous, and probably presented
no threat to her during her break from work, and she
was simply being polite. From the back, I'd certainly
appeared to her to be a manual worker – a stark
contrast to the bar's business suited patrons I noticed
with a little unease and embarrassment as I continued.
Then her PDA trilled. She read a message and called
the barkeeper over, asking for the screen above the bar
to be turned on. We watched in silence as footage of
the eater's attack formed a minute part of a news
bulletin. Then there followed a small clip, and I
recognised myself diving for cover as the eater was
obliterated behind me – that was great to see from a
different angle. She turned to me with recognition,
congratulating me with a pat on the shoulder before
turning on her stool to face me, asking me to continue
my story as she replaced her cup and saucer upon the
bar. The guy sitting to my right overheard me, and he
pulled his stool closer, waving a friend over a few
minutes later as he walked in. Before I knew it, I had
an audience – some staring in disbelief, others
checking my story with their PDA news feeds, nudging
and nodding to each other, calling friends, recording
me, taking shots. A few asked questions, most of
which I couldn't answer back then. Others offered me
transportation, but I insisted I would walk all the way

home. To this they responded with great respect and admiration. *"You're Gliese's walking man,"* someone shouted from the back of the group.

It soon became clear to me all these individuals were sadly strangers to me, and would remain so throughout the rest of my life. Such is the problem with a huge city and the population it contains, you'd be lucky to see the same person twice during your lifetime, unless, like a few there, I too became a regular at this bar. The girl remained seated at my side until she finished her lunch, then after a little while she checked her watch, reluctantly made her excuses and gradually disappeared through the semi-circle of voyeurs I'd attracted. My eyes followed her, and she turned, knowing my eyes were upon her above anyone else as she walked out of the doors and onto the busy street.

Circumstances had delivered me to this place and these people. We had all collided, and I wondered, if the eaters hadn't appeared, would I ever have met any of them during the usual pace of my life, would I ever meet any of them ever again? I decided no to both.

Slowly but surely the bar emptied as my story concluded for the third time. A few people shook my hand before departing, some bowed, some gave me their business cards. I was alone once more, so I paid my bill, left a tip and walked outside. Time was getting on, I needed to get home.

---

10. Requiem of Rainfall

Pale orange twilight settled in quickly as I walked, an all too brief prelude before the dark. I refused to take an automated transport, I wanted to walk away from what had happened, not be assisted. Walking was cathartic, although my joints began to ache, my sealed fractures throbbing a little with every step. The streets narrowed again, and I found myself beneath neon tubes, glass and coloured gases, signs in English, Russian, Mandarin and Urdu, animated illuminated figures above shop frontages enticing my fellow pedestrians inside. The pavement curved sharply up a gentle hill to the left, and as a fairly strong breeze blew down the street it carried newspaper pages curling around each other, caused chimes to sound as they hung from striped market stall awnings, flapping their farewells. Kids sped past on glidebikes as distant thunder crept across the rooftops, and the streets began to empty rapidly. Then the first droplets appeared, punctuating the background hum of electricity, faint music filtering out into the street from the tiny restaurants, where dim lights glowed orange behind thick leaded glass. At first, these tiny slivers of water created an uneven rhythm as they dampened the pavements in small dark spots. Then slowly the slivers grew, swept along by the wind as the thunder loomed closer. I huddled into a doorway to take shelter and looked up. The rain drifted in layered sheets, bouncing from the neon, momentarily absorbing the colours. Showers of yellow and blue and red, mid air fountains of orange and white cascading, spiralling and twisting in the air. A little way off to the north, a collection of narrow-field gravity tunnels were in operation, accepting produce and general supplies for the shops, restaurants and business of the district from delivery bots. The rain coursed through the tunnels, altered by their varied field strengths, slowed, forming larger droplets as the wind grew, creating a dozen different types of rain to extinguish the dryness of the streets and slanted rooftops. I stepped out to watch this hypnotic display, refreshed by the downpour upon my face, intrigued by this marvellous experience. It was then I was reminded of my own freefall, as millions of droplets were unleashed as if to mimic my past actions. The rhythm formed up as the rain grew heavier, every surface around me – myself included – became a percussive instrument, all part of this symphony, this requiem of rainfall. I found myself standing alone in the street, people wiping window condensation away, peering at this idiot happily becoming drenched before them, pressing their noses against the glass, their children pointing and tugging at their sleeves for an explanation. I smiled back to them all and walked on, refreshed, determined, the gutters coursing with rippling water reflecting the lights above, the drains quenched. The music of the streets became happier now, cohesive, focused into a steady cadence that lifted my spirits. Rain had never been so beautiful.

My thoughts returned to the woman at the bar (I hadn't even asked her name) and I wondered where she was now, what she was doing. If she was perhaps peering from a window and enjoying the sight too, or if she thought of me at all following our brief meeting. I lowered my head. Just a few more clicks now I estimated. I should be home by sunrise.

11. Homecoming

The morning was as bright as the day before and I shielded my eyes with a lazy saluting palm. The outer suburbs slept – it was a Saturday after all – with just a few vehicles crawling past me toward the centre of the city. It was going to be a warm day, streaks of thin white clouds highlighted with red. I was so damn tired, but I began to march, remembering my basic training of a few years ago. My heart began to pound with anticipation and I lifted my head, straightening my back with pride, allowing myself a satisfied smile behind the pain.

The silence around me was a little daunting, and I considered the possibility I'd wake up back in that ravine, that my journey had been nothing more than a drug induced forgery – my suit tricking me into self-belief, to drag me back to reality with a counterfeit memory of a future that *might* well be, whilst the drugs and nanites did their best to revive my shattered body to function. What better way to convince a broken man his life would, *could* continue if he wanted it to do so? For a moment I feared this to be true, that everything around me would evaporate, to reveal that craggy plain before me, and my journey would now have to be endured once again, but this time different. I imagined those chattering processors colluding with each other in a sub frequency I couldn't hear whilst I lay unconscious, hatching this plan – laughing at me, somehow communicating with and convincing my nanites this deception was for my own good and, ultimately, survival. I shook the paranoid possibility aside and looked to the curtained windows either side of the road, waiting for a reassuring telltale twitch, half a neighbour's face unable to quell their curiosity about this dishevelled individual.

Then I heard a dog bark in the distance, and I began to run, run through the pain that came again, my parents' house just around the next corner, nestled in a small cul-de-sac at the edge of this city. As I rounded the bend I stopped. Everyone was there waiting in the street, my friends, neighbours and, most importantly, my parents. They all cheered as they saw me, punching the air for my triumph. My mother and father ran to me, my mother almost knocking me to the ground as we embraced in tears. I was home.

A debrief later that morning from a rather stuffy box-ticking suited individual took just an hour or so, and following a shower and a meal I slept for the remainder of the day. The following Monday, taking a week's break, I ventured back into Gliesia's centre, via a transport this time. A medical check gave me the all clear, providing me with new nanites (the one and only time this has been sanctioned, I believe). I bought a new guitar and I found myself looking for somewhere to eat lunch. The choice was obvious, and I took that same stool at the bar early once again, waiting for one particular member of the lunchtime crowd to arrive.

My great grandson remained impassive for a little while, sitting there, mulling over everything I'd told him.

"So," he finally said with a grin, "did this woman appear at the bar?"

I picked up my knife and fork, checking them for stains, which I knew wouldn't be there. I replaced them slowly and clasped my hands together on the table before me. "Of course she did." I nodded toward the kitchen, "And now she's just about to serve dinner." I unfolded a napkin and placed it on my lap, then poured the lemon tea for the three of us. "Following our meal, you can tell us all about what you've been doing these past few days." I grinned without looking up. "Obviously over a nice, long walk."

Howard Watts is a writer, artist and composer living in Seaford who also provides the wraparound cover art for this issue. His artwork can be seen in its native resolution on his deviantart page: hswatts.deviantart.com. His novel The Master of Clouds is now available on Kindle.

The Quarterly Review

Reviews by
Stephen Theaker,
Douglas J. Ogurek,
Jacob Edwards
and Rafe McGregor

Douglas J. Ogurek's work has appeared in the BFS Journal, The Literary Review, Morpheus Tales, Gone Lawn, and several anthologies. He lives in a Chicago suburb with the woman whose husband he is and their pit bull Phlegmpus Bilesnot. Douglas's website can be found at: www.douglasjogurek.weebly.com.

Jacob Edwards also writes 42-word reviews for Derelict Space Sheep. This writer, poet and recovering lexiphanicist's website is at www.jacobedwards.id.au. He has a Facebook page at www.facebook. com/JacobEdwardsWriter, where he posts poems and the occasional oddity, and he can now be found on Twitter too: https://twitter.com/ToastyVogon.

*Rafe McGregor has published over one
hundred and twenty short stories, novellas,
magazine articles, journal papers, and
review essays. His work includes crime
fiction, weird tales, military history,
literary criticism, and academic philosophy.*

*Stephen Theaker's reviews have appeared
in Interzone, Black Static, Prism and the
BFS Journal, as well as clogging up our
pages. He shares his home with three
slightly smaller Theakers, runs the British
Fantasy Awards (for the rest of the month),
and works in legal and medical publishing.*

Audio

Alien: Out of the Shadows, by Tim Lebbon and Dirk Maggs (Audible Originals)

This full cast audio interquel places itself between two
of the greatest science fiction films of all time, *Alien*
and *Aliens*. That takes a good deal of ambition, but,
then, it is adapted from Tim Lebbon's novel by Dirk
Maggs, whose CV, taking in everyone from Superman
to Arthur Dent, shows he is not afraid of a challenge.
We join Ellen Ripley (played here by Laurel Lefkow),
sole human survivor of the *Nostromo*, as she records a
message for her daughter and settles down for
hypersleep. What she, and we, didn't realise at the end
of *Alien* was that murderous company android Ash
had uploaded his consciousness to the escape pod's
computer. He hasn't given up on his mission, and
what's worse he now sounds just like Rutger Hauer,
having scraped together a new voice from what's
available in the computer system. He changes their

course, taking them to LV178, a mining planet where he suspects the alien xenomorphs might be found. And he's right. The miners disturbed something on that planet, and now, like Dracula coming to Whitby, it's on its way up to the orbiting *Marion* in a shuttle. Chief engineer Chris Hooper (played by Corey Johnson) and the other surviving miners will need the help of Ripley if any of them are to survive, but the presence of Ash is just going to make things worse.

As well as the films, there have been a lot of good Aliens comics and games, and this adaptation shows how extremely well suited they are to the audio medium too, despite being fairly quiet, as monsters go. Characters talk over comms as they explore locations where the aliens might be lurking, and of course comms cut out as the aliens attack, creating a tension reminiscent of *Journey into Space* at its most

frightening. The plot gives the characters some very difficult decisions to make, so the conversations never feel redundant. The record entries of the disembodied Ash are used cleverly to make sure listeners know exactly what's going on in each of the ten chapters. (The Audible app's new clips feature helps with this too.) One problem listeners may have is that a lot of what Ripley sees in this story seems to come as a surprise to her in the second film. Are we supposed to think that she kept that essential information from the colonial marines? Or is this a new timeline, branching off before *Aliens*? The story does answer these questions by the end, but not really in a way that'll have anyone cheering. Nevertheless, this is a good, solid four-and-a-half-hour alien adventure that sounds terrific. It should satisfy anyone with a hankering for more of the galaxy's second meanest bipeds. *Stephen Theaker* ★★★☆☆

Books

Archivist Wasp, by Nicole Kornher-Stace (Big Mouth House)

It is a truth universally acknowledged that the best way to begin a novel is with a fight to the death, and that is how this novel begins. Wasp is the current archivist, her job being to capture ghosts and record what information she can glean from them. This miserable and lonely existence has a downside: each year she is challenged by three upstarts to a knife fight. If one of them wins, they'll become the archivist, and she'll become a ghost. If she wins, she has to tie a braid of their hair into her own, making her head heavier by the year, giving her headaches, making it more likely that she will lose to the children.

Wasp is sixteen years old, and doesn't expect to live much longer. However, she survives the book's opening duel, just barely, and after a period of convalescence returns to the job. A very strong ghost appears, one who can harm her, speak to her, even heal her bad ankle, and he wants her to come with him to where the ghosts live, in search of a woman he loved in life, and has never been able to find in death.

★ "A ravishing, profane, and bittersweet post-apocalyptic bildungsroman transcends genre into myth."
Kirkus Reviews (starred review)

ARCHIVIST
WASP
A NOVEL
NICOLE
KORNHER-STACE

Good mysteries and good fights are two things I really like in a book, and *Archivist Wasp* delivers in both respects. Wasp is resilient and resourceful, and likely to win the admiration of all readers, not to mention their sympathy, and the same goes for her ghost, whose pre-apocalyptic story is not quite what I was expecting. Another terrific title from Small Beer Press, and clearly an author to look out for too. *Stephen Theaker* ★★★★☆

The Devil's Detective, by Simon Kurt Unsworth (Del Rey)

Back in issue twenty-four, I reviewed Mark Valentine's *The Black Veil and Other Tales of Supernatural Sleuths* (2008), an anthology that has since come to define the specific area of overlap between crime fiction and speculative fiction known as either the *supernatural sleuth* or the *occult detective*. In his introduction, Valentine explains how the magazine contributors of the late nineteenth century began to explore different ways in which the relatively new and incredibly popular figure of the private detective could be merged with the much older but still entertaining milieu of the ghost story. This combination of detective protagonist and ghostly setting saw the initial blossoming of the subgenre, which included such greats as Arthur Machen's Mr Dyson, Robert Eustace and L.T. Meade's John Bell, E. and H. Heron's Flaxman Low (the Herons were actually the Prichards, a mother and son team), Algernon Blackwood's Dr John Silence, and William Hope Hodgson's Carnacki.

The particular and peculiar mix of genres embodied by the occult detective made the transition from short stories to television in the second half of the twentieth century with *Adam Adamant Lives!* (1966–1967), *Randall and Hopkirk (Deceased)* (1969–1971, remade in

2000–2001), and *Kolchak: The Night Stalker* (1974–1975, remade in 2005). The recent revival of the subgenre was perhaps most firmly established with *The X-Files* (1993–2002), the tenth season of which was released earlier this year, coinciding with both the fifth season of *Grimm* and the third season of *Penny Dreadful*. The

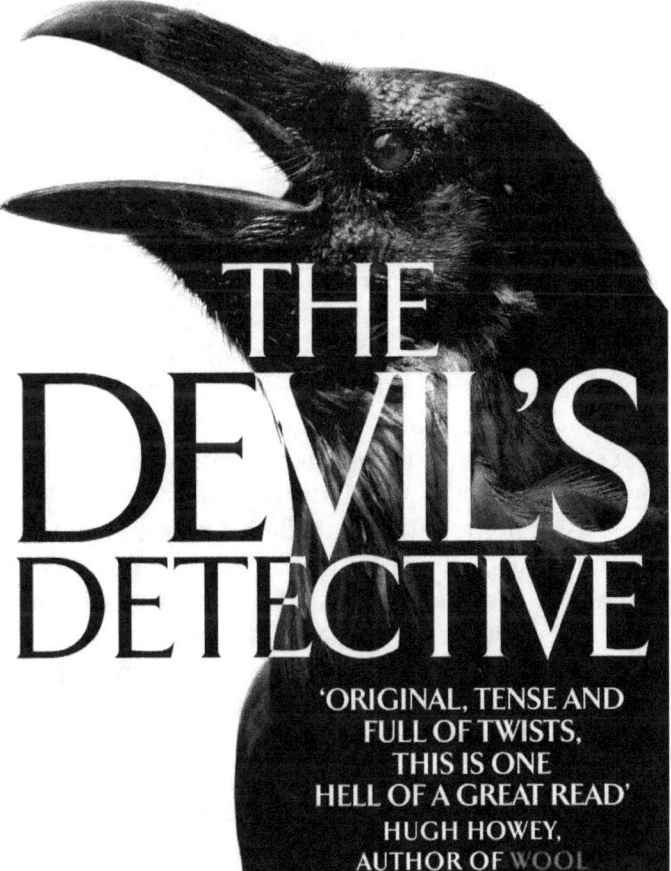

SIMON KURT UNSWORTH

THE DEVIL'S DETECTIVE

'ORIGINAL, TENSE AND
FULL OF TWISTS,
THIS IS ONE
HELL OF A GREAT READ'
HUGH HOWEY,
AUTHOR OF WOOL

graphic novel has been especially influential in maintaining the public's interest, with two particularly long-running series standing out, *Hellblazer* (beginning in 1988) and *Hellboy* (beginning in 1993). Strangely, there has been less of an interest in the occult detective in mainstream novels, although three long-running series characters have emerged. Jim Butcher's Harry Dresden was introduced in 2000 and the fifteenth Dresden File was published in 2014. John Connolly's Charlie Parker was introduced in 1999 and his fourteenth case was published this year – although I have reservations as to whether Parker can accurately be called an occult detective (see my review of his thirteenth case, *A Song of Shadows*, in this issue). Phil Rickman's Merrily Watkins series began in 1998, with her thirteenth investigation published at the end of last year. The popularity of the occult detective is further evinced by the many failed and few successful attempts to combine Sherlock Holmes and the Cthulhu Mythos and the fact that a large minority – if not the majority – of new Holmes stories are works of speculative fiction rather than crime fiction.

One of the reasons for this popularity is that the subgenre has the potential to literally offer the best of both worlds, combining the cognitive demands of a clever mystery with the emotive atmosphere of a frightful horror story. What distinguishes the occult detective story from the crime fiction subgenre of the psychological thriller – the work of, for example, Thomas Harris, Mo Hayder, and Steve Mosby – is that there is at least the possibility of a genuine supernatural element. In the short story form, this introduces an extra element of suspense in that some cases have natural solutions and others supernatural solutions and Hodgson exploited this duality brilliantly with Carnacki (albeit briefly, courtesy of his death on the Western Front in 1918). The essence of the occult detective story is a mystery that must be solved by means mundane or magical in a setting that is either real or fantastic, with all possible permutations of this basic formula permitted. Whichever option the author selects, he or she faces the tricky task of relatively quickly establishing the internal logic of the almost-real or unreal world in order that the reader can play the mystery game, which is usually the game of working out who the killer is.

Simon Kurt Unsworth has opted for a fantasy world, a post-*Paradise Lost* Hell where there is a truce between God and Satan, and his detective is Thomas Fool, one of Hell's three Information Men (one of whom is a woman). The Information Men are the only police in Hell and no more than three are required because their job is simply to record demonic crimes against humanity rather than investigate them. *The Devil's Detective* (368pp, £5.99) begins with Fool on escort duty, responsible for the safety of a delegation from Heaven which is negotiating with the (Infernal) Bureaucracy for human souls. My sole criticism of the work is that its thematic content remains opaque throughout. What, I wondered – and still do – is really driving the plot forward? There are several fascinating options: the world-mapping of a new Hell where humans serve demons for all eternity in an amicable equilibrium with Heaven; the solution to the mystery of the murder of a human prostitute in this occult setting; a morality tale describing a Hell that is characterised by the absence of free will for its human occupants; or an allegory that is either pro- or anti-religion describing how human beings have already built Hell on Earth or how ridiculous the conception of an afterlife is. All of these disparate strands run through the narrative, though there is little to unify them.

Aside from the ingenuity of the setting and the way in which the rules of the mystery game played in Hell are established without resorting to lengthy swathes of exposition, the quality of Unsworth's writing reaches outstanding heights at times. An example is the death of one of the main characters, who is accosted by a group of minor antagonists that gradually becomes more and more dangerous until one suddenly realises that he (or *she*, I'll avoid spoilers) is in mortal danger. The brilliance of this particular piece is in the way in which Unsworth somehow manages to combine the pace and tension of the thriller with the slow-building apprehension of horror and he is both competent and comfortable with a foot in each genre. Ultimately, and this is why Fool is such a fine example of the occult detective, the novel works well as a traditional murder mystery because there are just enough clues for the reader to realise that he or she could have worked out the solution had they paid more attention to detail as well as the link between plot and subplot that is *de rigueur*.

Returning to my criticism about thematic content, the question I wanted answered was not the identity of what soon emerges as a serial killer in Hell, but the whereabouts of Satan. What, post-war, is he up to? There is a suggestion that he has retired to Crow Heights, a kind of gated community where the ancient and powerful have locked themselves away, but the truth is more interesting and – along with the final twist of the narrative – sets up a fascinating milieu for the rest of the series. The Old Hell was fire and brimstone, the New Hell was chaos and uncertainty for its human citizenry, but following Fool's interest in actually solving crimes, the Hell of the future is a Hell with a completely powerful and entirely unaccountable police force. The mysteries of this forthcoming Hell will be revealed in *The Devil's Evidence*, due for publication in October. *Rafe McGregor*

Kalpa Imperial, by Angela Gorodischer (Small Beer Press)

Subtitled "the greatest empire that never was", this book tells a series of stories about the long-lived empire of Kalpa – or so we presume, since that name only appears in the title. In the book it is just the Empire, and it has a north, and a less easily governed south, and it has lasted (or will last: some stories hint that this is a future empire) so long that emperors and

even dynasties may be completely unknown to their successors. Some stories, like "The Old Incense Road", about an elderly man leading traders across the desert, take place over a shortish span of time, but others are rather more expansive, like the remarkable "And the Streets Deserted", which follows a city from its founding and shows its many different lives, as an imperial capital, as a home for artists, as a spa for the unwell. Each story brings a majesty to the lives great and small that it examines, and each is equally enjoyable. The rule in the Empire is much like that for the original run of Star Trek films, that emperors will, in general, alternate between the good and the bad, and the book shows us both. The wisdom and determination of the Great Empress Abderjhalda in "Portrait of the Empress" or the emperor who never leaves his bedroom in "The Two Hands" are an example of each. The book was originally published in two volumes in Argentina in 1983, and this translation by Ursula K. Le Guin, which seems, so far as one can tell without reading the original, to be impeccably done, is from 2003. It should appeal to anyone with a taste for the epic, and in particular readers who enjoyed Lucius Shepard's *The Dragon Griaule*, with which it shares many similarities: of tone, structure, and indeed quality. *Stephen Theaker* ★★★★★

King Wolf, by Steven Savile (Fox Spirit Books)

A collection of three short stories, written years apart from each other, but sharing a common link. "The Fragrance of You" is about an illustrator, Jon Sieber, who falls in love with the daughter of the writer Hoke Berglund, author of such strange works as *Princess Scapegoat*, *The Forgetting Wood* and *Angel Home*, after meeting her at the old man's funeral. As his feelings for her deepens, he becomes increasingly bothered by her habit of sneaking out in the middle of the night. Eventually he makes the mistake of following her... "All That Remains Is You" then takes us back to meet the writer Hoke Berglund when he was still alive, and preparing to pitch his second book to a publisher. It's a book that deals with the loss of his wife, the birth of his daughter, and his own institutionalisation – not exactly the stuff of a

licensing extravaganza, but the hype machine is up and running before Hoke even steps into his publisher's office. On his way in he is stopped by an older man who begs him not to publish the book, for the sake of his daughter. But in the meeting he "signed what they wanted him to sign and walked out feeling uncomfortably like Marlowe's Dr. Faustus". The third story, "Remembering You, Forgetting Me", was written a decade later and appears for the first time in this book. We return to Jon Sieber, attending something like an alcoholics anonymous meeting, having drunk himself silly for seven years after the events of "The Fragrance of You". He tells them what he found hidden in the last seven interviews of Hoke Berglund: a terrible accusation... The book ends with an afterword placing the stories in the context of the actual author's own life, not normally something I enjoy, but it seems appropriate in this case, after reading a set of stories that are, in my view, all about the relationship between the author, and his or her characters, and the reader. The book shows us Mr. Self Affliction, a disgusting creature who pours his words into others so that they can speak as if human; a self-lacerating view of a writer's job, though perhaps balanced by the in-joke of having a character wonder if their story was being "written around me by the master storyteller". Writers create fake people, and by the magic of literature we fall in love with them, or at least feel for them, as Savile makes us do here so brilliantly. *Stephen Theaker*
★★★★☆

The Last Weekend, by Nick Mamatas
(PS Publishing)

Even before the collapse, Vasilis Kostopolos was not a nice guy, and not a happy guy either. A self-loathing alcoholic who follows an ex-girlfriend to Boston, who follows random women on the subway while abusing them in his mind, who doesn't mind if the money he spends on drink helps fund the IRA, he ends up in San Francisco, a surprisingly good place to be when the dead start to rise. There are no cemeteries there, and the zombies struggle with the big hills. He's a writer, and he can prove that with the print-out of his one published story that he keeps in his pocket at all

times, but he takes a job as a driller. When the dying seem likely to turn, he gets a call. If he's lucky, he gets there once they're dead but before they've revived, but he's rarely lucky. Turns out he's pretty good at the job, or at least he doesn't quit or get eaten. He's a guy who spent his "adult life trying to avoid adult life, living a simplified version of it without dreams of a family". Before the collapse he would consider killing himself "a dozen times a day, maybe more". So when everything falls apart for everyone else (at least in the USA; nowhere else seems to be affected) he copes pretty well, his life hasn't got much worse. (Also a theme of the later show *Fear the Walking Dead*, where a junkie adapts better to the apocalypse than the rest of his family.) He even starts to meet women: Alexa, who shoots a boy who jumps out at them, pretending to be a zombie; Thunder, a friend of the dead boy who shamelessly steals Vasilis's stuff; Jaffe, a civil servant who kept on serving after the collapse. Thunder and Alexa share a desire to get to the bottom of things, to uncover the mysteries of the apocalypse, to find out what the government (such as it is) is hiding, and Vassily gets mixed up in their plans despite himself. This is a terrific book, the kind of thing you might expect if McSweeney's had a horror imprint, intelligent, provoking, self-aware, and full of interesting ideas. You wouldn't ever want to be this guy, as a writer, or as a human being, but you can understand why he survives, and why it takes the breakdown of human society for him to write his great American novel. *Stephen Theaker* ★★★★☆

**A Song of Shadows, by John Connolly
(Hodder & Stoughton)**

A Song of Shadows (464pp, £3.85) is the thirteenth "Charlie Parker thriller", as the series is described by

Hodder & Stoughton, first published in hardback in 2015. First and foremost – and quite possibly *because of* rather than *in spite of* the criticisms I shall make – the series is extremely successful, regularly ranking high on various bestseller lists and regularly receiving rave ratings from the most trusted crime fiction reviewers. I must confess to not having read all of Parker's cases, which began with *Every Dead Thing* in 1999 (and was, as an example of my previous claim, the *L.A. Times* Book of the Year), but I have read the first two and most recent two and can confirm that there has been no fluctuation in quality. Connolly is not one of those writers who rests on his laurels, resorts to repeated uses of the same formula, or tires of his protagonist. My gripe, and I think it is more than mere whimsy on my part, is the idiosyncratic mix of crime and horror Connolly has weaved around Parker.

In his helpful guide to the series on the *Crime Fiction Lover* website, David Prestidge writes that: "The books are peopled with genuinely mean human criminal types, but Connolly introduces supernatural foes in the novels as well." The books are billed as *dark crime fiction* in the same way that *dark fantasy* is now a distinct subcategory of the fantasy genre. To sacrifice accuracy for brevity, dark crime fiction is crime fiction written by a horror writer or a mystery told as a horror story or crime fiction that gestures towards but does not quite cross over into horror fiction... basically, a crime fiction series that is situated just *this* side of the *crime*–horror border. The two genres are, of course, complementary to a great extent and it is no surprise that Edgar Allan Poe was such an important figure for both, that Conan Doyle's *The Hound of the Baskervilles* is billed as both a great crime story and a great horror story, or that may of H.P. Lovecraft's weird tales take investigators of some sort as their protagonists.

Prestidge continues: "Yet he never uses the paranormal to explain away loopholes in the plot."

The issue isn't using the para-normal to fill normal loopholes in the plot, but rather integrating the mystery and horror elements of the narrative such that they complement rather than counteract one another and this is where several weaknesses emerge. First, the books are longer than most mystery novels, the length exacerbated by the often slow and leisurely build-up to the main plot. This would not be problematic were the denouement worth the wait, i.e. a clever or original mix of mystery and magic, sleuthing and the supernatural. But, as Prestidge correctly notes: "There aren't any [loopholes], and the Charlie Parker books all offer solid and original mysteries. He is a PI, after all." Crime fiction readers, particularly those who prefer "thrillers" to "mysteries" are accustomed to fast-paced plots and the slower the action, the more drama they demand in the climax. The fact that all supernatural elements are always (at least in the four I have read and according to Prestidge) peripheral to the main plot – always, in other words, a subplot at best – makes me think of the series as crime-dressed-up-as-horror – in a pejorative *sheep-in-wolf's-clothing* sense. Parker's living daughter (Sam) can see the dead and sense evil and the spirit of his dead daughter (Jennifer) communicates with both him and Sam in *A Song of Shadows*. There are at least two events in the novel – a young girl sleepwalking and the earth opening up under a villain – that are presented as supernatural, but then quickly rationalised (as the dream of a young girl with a neurological disease and as a rare but not improbable geological phenomenon respectively). I found the subsequent debunking of these at times gripping supernatural scenes something of an anti-climax and that term really sums up my whole experience of the book.

Connolly takes a big risk with his villains in using war criminals from the Second World War. Assuming that the events of the narrative are supposed to be contemporary (there is nothing to suggest otherwise) and that National Socialist Germany *in extremis* may have used sixteen-year-olds as concentration camp

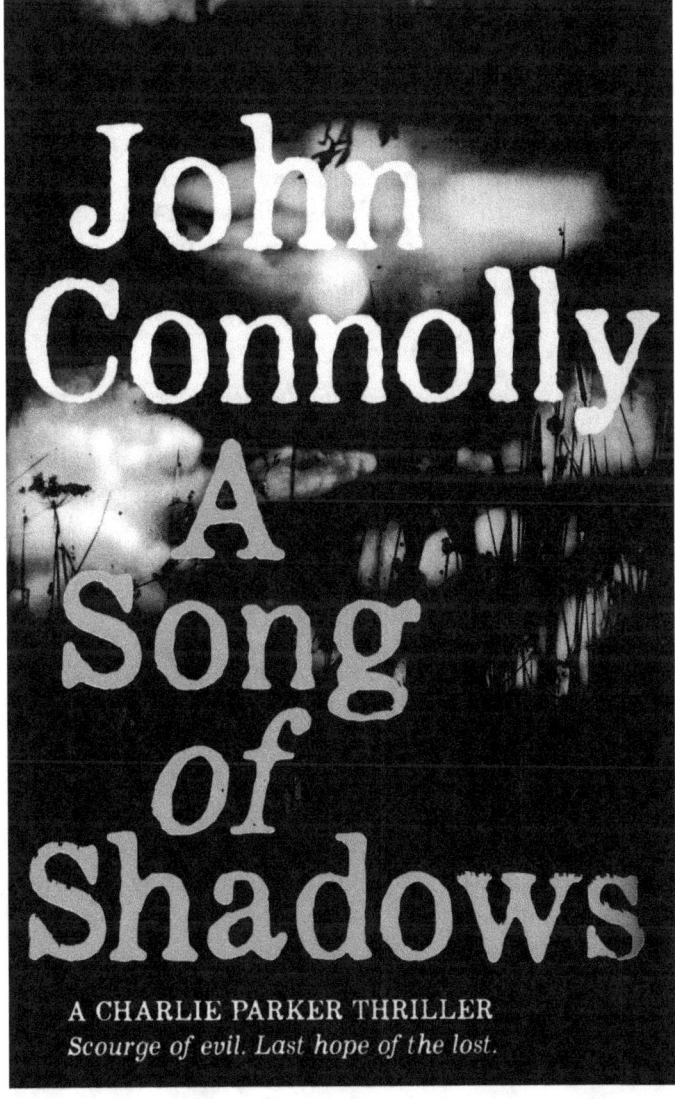

John Connolly

A Song of Shadows

A CHARLIE PARKER THRILLER

Scourge of evil. Last hope of the lost.

guards – and granting that the camps were maintained until the very end of the war – the youngest possible war criminal would be eighty-six. Given the separation of the supernatural from the main plot, the criminals involved are men rather than demons and eighty-six-year-old men are not very frightening – unless, of course, they are million- or billion-aires at the head of a new evil empire. The Nazi-turned-businessman is something of a cliché, but in avoiding the cliché Connolly presents his readers with a group of evil old men doddering around New England, unworthy antagonists for super-sleuth Parker even if he is recovering from the multiple wounds sustained in his previous case. What makes this even worse for me is that the revelation of the main villain occurs relatively early on (for a mystery, that is), which once again creates a sense of... anti-climax.

Connolly's fans – and there are dozens, probably hundreds, of thousands of them – may well think I haven't read the book because Goodreads (to name but one forum) has many reviewers writing about the suspense being maintained to the last page and the jaw-dropping conclusion. I think I know what they have in mind, but I am baffled that it should generate such excitement. And yes, I have read all four books carefully from first page to last. Parker is a likeable sort of chap who leads an interesting sort of life, but neither Parker nor his life justifies the many hundreds of pages that each case generates. As mystery stories, the series is far too slow-paced; as horror stories, the continual and continued relegation of the supernatural to the side-line is disappointing; as a combination of mystery and horror, I can't help but feel that a writer of Connolly's undoubted skill could have merged a hardboiled PI with a setting that is both gritty and realistic on the one hand and populated by the angels and demons which the series often promises but never delivers on the other. It is only the worry that I have missed some obvious virtue of the novels that kept me coming back, but I'm afraid I've decided that life is too short to attempt a fifth... I'm sure Parker and Connolly will both do fine without me. *Rafe McGregor*

Songs of a Dead Dreamer and Grimscribe, by Thomas Ligotti (Penguin Classics)

In issue forty-nine I reviewed Thomas Ligotti's *The Spectral Link* (2014) and described him as the *most accomplished* practitioner of weird fiction today. As such, it is satisfying to see that he has finally been admitted to the canon of twentieth century horror fiction by inclusion in the Penguin Classics series, which has recently taken an interesting turn with the publication of relatively obscure works of classic pulp horror fiction, like Clark Ashton Smith's *The Dark Eidolon and Other Fantasies* (2014). This is particularly satisfying in Ligotti's case as although he is in his fourth decade of publishing to great critical acclaim, he has failed to achieve mainstream success – understood in terms of mass market paperback sales. I think there are two reasons for this: although he has published sixteen books to date (excluding the Penguin release, but not *The Spectral Link*), they have all been collections of short stories, short novellas, or poetry rather than the novel so beloved by commercial publishers. Second, there is the – and I know no better term – *weirdness* of the stories themselves, which I imagine will not have an appeal beyond horror aficionados in the way that, for example, Stephen King's work does. Ligotti has nonetheless remained a firm favourite of a limited audience and I was lucky enough to pick up Volume 9, Number 1 (1989) of the long-abandoned *Crypt of Cthulhu* magazine, with nine

short pieces by him, at a recent book fair. The price
was very reasonable – *too* reasonable – and I wish
there was more demand for his work.

Penguin have overcome the problem of the public's
preference for substantial volumes by compiling
Ligotti's first two short story collections for their
series. *Songs of a Dead Dreamer* was first published in

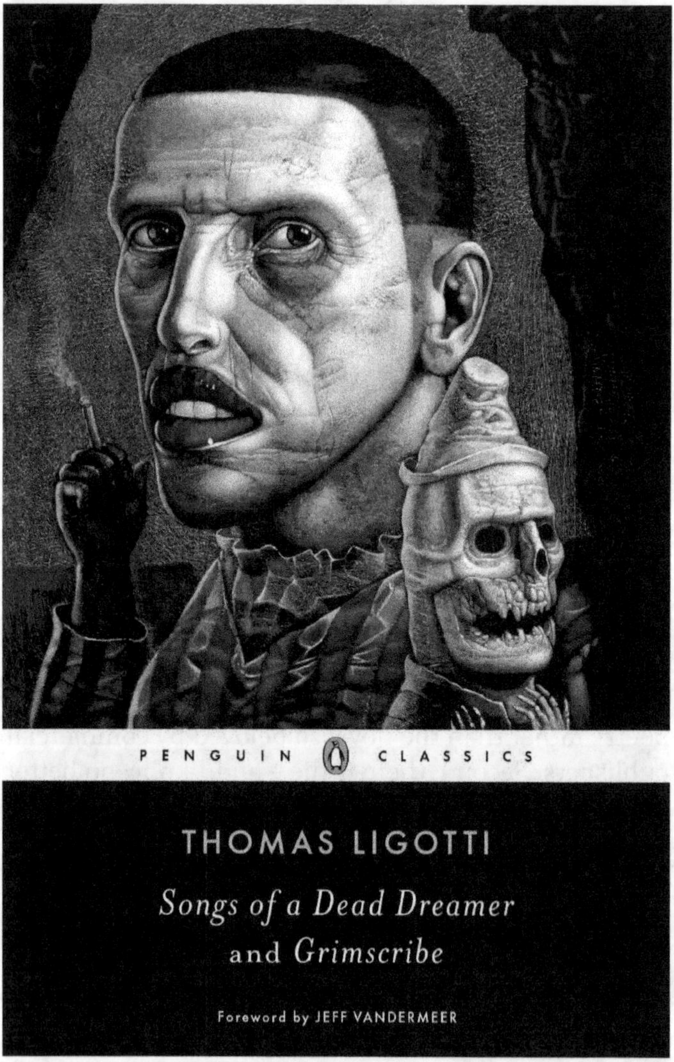

PENGUIN CLASSICS

THOMAS LIGOTTI

Songs of a Dead Dreamer
and *Grimscribe*

Foreword by JEFF VANDERMEER

1985 and contains nineteen stories and a curious (but fascinating) lecture; *Grimscribe* was first published in 1991 and contains thirteen stories and an (also curious but fascinating) introduction for a total of thirty-four short works preceded by a foreword from Jeff VanderMeer. VanderMeer is best known for his Ambergris and Southern Reach series and, with his wife Ann, as the foremost anthologist of weird fiction in the twenty-first century. The foreword is everything one would hope from a preface: laudatory without being slavish and informative without being pedantic. VanderMeer is quick to mention "the author's unique way of seeing the world", which is precisely the reason I differ from him in my description of Ligotti as a writer of weird tales. VanderMeer sees Ligotti as "always *passing through*" the weird to the literary, but I do not consider classification as both weird (understood as a subgenre of horror) and literary as incompatible, even if Ligotti's work is uniquely classified as such.

In my previous review, I focused on two themes explored by Ligotti: the difference between things as they really are and things as we perceive them and the sinister implications of the meaning of "demoralization". The first story in the collection, "The Frolic", evinces both of these, but it is the former that has the greater resonance in Ligotti's *oeuvre*. In my review of David Tallerman's *The Sign in the Moonlight and Other Stories* (2016) in issue fifty-five, I mentioned S.T. Joshi's definition of weird fiction as embodying a distinctive world-view by the author. There is a sense in which Ligotti's distinctive world-view is one that explores the deconstructive criticism that was so popular and so infamous towards the end of the last century. There has been a great deal of nonsense written about (and some would say *by*) Jacques Derrida, who popularised the approach in the sixties, but the basic idea behind deconstruction is simple: human beings (subjective experience) can only gain access to the real world (objective reality) through concepts, which are articulated through language. The worry, which stems from curiosities such as the fact that languages not only use different words for the same concept, but have different concepts that cannot be translated in their entirety, is that no human language and therefore no human conception maps perfectly on to reality. There is obviously plenty of overlap – otherwise we would not be able to build bridges, cure diseases, invent the internet, and fly to the moon – but there is no identity relation between concept and reality. The space that this opens up is the difference between the world as we think it is and the world as it really is, where aspects of the latter are understood to remain permanently inaccessible to us. Ligotti takes this difference and scrapes away at it, making it larger and more frightening. In "The Frolic", a prison psychologist states of his paedophile patient: "He says he just made the evidence look that way for the dull masses, that what he really means by 'frolicking' is a type of activity quite different from, even opposed to, the crimes for which he was convicted." The actions of the patient are even more horrific than they initially appear for they are not only a form of torture, but a reminder that we live in a world that we are incapable of fully understanding.

One of the features of deconstructive criticism is that it undermines commonly accepted logic and Ligotti's tales follow suit. A basic principle of logic, for example, is the law of noncontradiction, which states that something cannot be both true and false at the same time, but the narrator of "The Frolic" demurs: "'It's as if I know something and don't know it at the same time.'" He is subsequently shown to both know and not know – knowing where the evidence points and also knowing that his grasp of reality is subjective rather than objective. And later, from "Dream of a Manikin": "Accredited studies notwithstanding – as I'm sure you would contest – suppose the dreamer is not a man or butterfly, but both ... or neither, something else altogether." This is the most distinctive and the most disturbing element of Ligotti's horror, the way it deconstructs reality in the philosophical sense. Even if we have good mental health, reality is revealed only through fallible conceptions and this lack of fit between words and world is a frightening subject of contemplation, a gap through which monsters of all kinds can enter. It is not that Ligotti's monsters are more frightening than those of other authors, but that he exposes our world as a place that remains essentially – necessarily – unknown to us and, as H.P. Lovecraft proclaimed in "Supernatural Horror in Literature" (1927), there is nothing more frightening than the unknown.

The influence of Lovecraft is strongly felt in many, if not most, of these stories – but this is a genuine influence, of his cosmic futilitarianism rather than his strangely named gods and books. Occasionally, it is explicit: the end of "The Last Feast of Harlequin" reveals the story's dedication to Lovecraft and is a re-writing of "The Festival" (1925) without that story's flaws (and also acknowledges the influence of Edgar Allan Poe with mention of "the Conqueror Worm"). Mostly, the influence is implicit, from the suggestion of an alien presence in "The Frolic" to the distant similarities between "The Dreaming in Nortown" and "The Shadow Out of Time" (1936) and the more obvious similarities between "The Shadow at the Bottom of the World" and "The Colour Out of Space" (1927). The latter story by Ligotti, the last in *Grimscribe*, is particularly interesting in that it throws up one of the two major differences between Ligotti and his predecessor: Ligotti is not only a much better writer than Lovecraft, but where Lovecraft was fascinated by rural and far-flung locales, Ligotti's focus is on urban settings. This choice makes his writing even more unnerving for it is in the towns and cities, where we have self-evidently shaped reality to our own ends, that we should feel most at home in the world – but where the cracks between perception and reality are at their widest. *Rafe McGregor*

Travel Light, by Naomi Mitchison (Small Beer Press)

Little baby Halla has the misfortune to be a fairy tale princess, of the sort whose mother has passed away and father has remarried. The new queen wants her killed, but luckily the baby's nurse Matulli is from Finmark, and has the unusual knack of being able to turn herself into a bear. This she does, and carries the baby away into "the deep dark woods where the rest of the bears were waking up from their winter sleep". She lives with the bear cubs, learning to appreciate the taste of crunched mice, and the way the forest speaks in smells to the bears. She spends much of her later youth living with a friendly dragon, and comes to see the world from a dragon's point of view, where maidens are thoughtfully offered for dinner, and heroes interfere with everyone's best interests, and kings squander the gold that dragons sensibly gather together. When her stay with the dragon comes to an end, her voyage begins, taking her all the way to Constantinople to meet the Emperor. The book gets a little drier here, less whimsical, more political, and this, plus a certain amount of threatened and implied sexual violence, may explain why it did not become the famous children's classic posited in the introduction. The way it approaches the hypocrisy of the established church is well done, but maybe not

"Disarmingly familiar: like a memory only half-recalled. You will love this book."
—Holly Black (author of *Valiant* and The Spiderwick Chronicles)

Travel Light

Naomi Mitchison

Author of *The Corn King and the Spring Queen*

where readers might have hoped it would go after starting off with bears and dragons and a valkyrie. But it is still a very good book, one that plays clever games with defamiliarization, perception and time, and it lets its princess heroine decide for herself, a half century before *Frozen* and *Princeless*, whether her particular destiny was to marry or not. *Stephen Theaker*

★★★★☆

Comics

Fall of Cthulhu Omnibus, by Michael Alan Nelson, Mateus Santolouco and chums (Boom! Studios)

This huge book collects six trade paperbacks in one epic volume. The first five stories, from "The Fugue" through to "Apocalypse", concern the plans of Nyarlathotep, the creeping chaos, who has taken human form and resurrected Abdul Alhazred to write a new chapter of the *Necronomicon*, a chapter concerning the fate of Cthulhu, who sleeps undying under the waves in R'lyeh. A saga that ends with gods clashing and the Dreamlands spilling their nightmares upon the earth begins in a more mundane setting, with Cy and his girlfriend Jordan at a cafe, where Cy's uncle, Professor Walt McKinley of Miskatonic University, shows up, rambling about the blood on his hands before taking his own life, right there, al fresco. He leaves Cy a big bundle of mysteries and a knife ornamented with eyes that follow you around the room. It's the start of a story that will take Cy to the traditional Lovecraftian edge of madness and a long way beyond. He will meet allies, like Sheriff Raymond Dirk, whose family have long tried to keep the craziness in Arkham from bubbling malevolently to the surface, and Luci Jenifer Inacio das Neves, or Lucifer for short, a teenage rascal with a pretty decent handle on what is going on. The three of them will encounter nightmares and gods, monsters of all kinds, most startlingly of all the Harlot, who summons unhappy men to the Dreamlands and gives them what they want, for a horrible price. A variety of artists take turns to portray this amazing colossal woman as we pass through the book's six hundred pages, and each captures her horror in a differently spectacular way.

The sixth section of the book is in part an ironic
epilogue, but mostly a prequel, showing what went
down (if you'll forgive me) in Atlantis long ago.
Overall, this is a good solid attempt at a Cthulhu
mythos comic book, very much in the style of what
you might expect from an official TV adaptation of

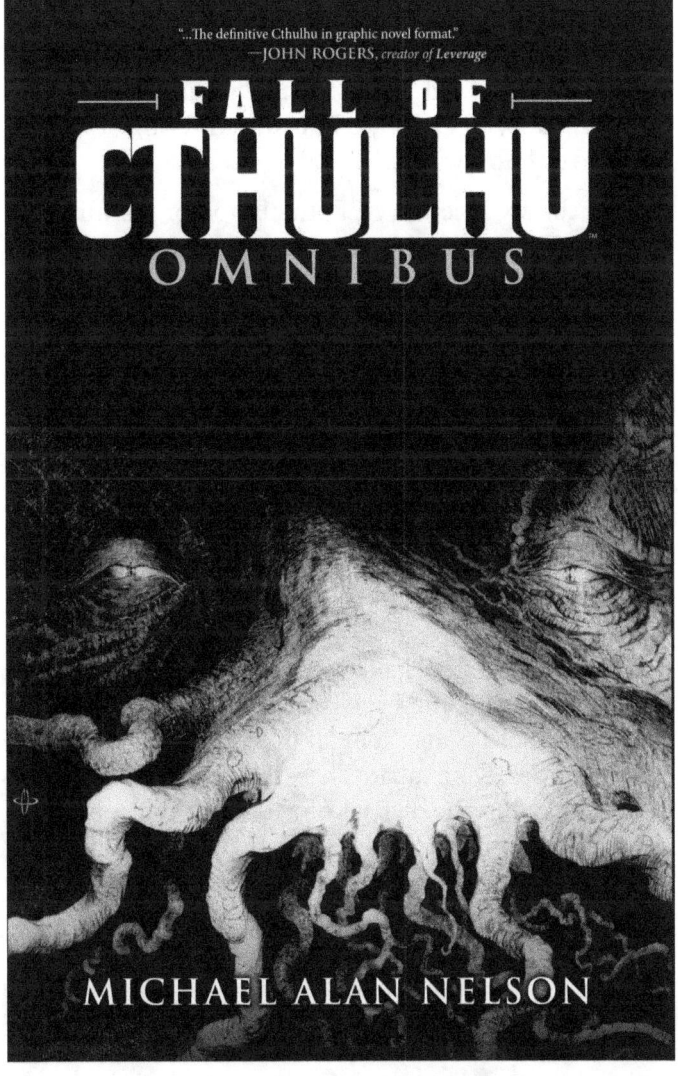

Lovecraft's work, rather than the glancing references and nods we so often get. The scenes in the Dreamlands are the high points, different artists and art styles used to render their strangeness. Cthulhu's name is in the title, but this is about the Harlot and Nyarlathotep and the humans caught in the middle of their battle. You wouldn't want to be in their shoes when R'lyeh starts to rise... *Stephen Theaker* ★★★★☆

The Hounds of Hell, Book 1: The Eagle's Companions, by Philippe Thirault and Christian Højgaard (Humanoids)

During the sixth century CE, the Emperor Justinian reigns in Byzantium, but dreams of reclaiming the western Roman empire, which has fallen to the barbarians. Angles and Saxons here in the UK, Vandals in Corsica and North Africa, Visigoths in Spain, and Ostrogoths in Italy: Theodoric, king of the Goths, has been named imperial regent. Justinian's young wife, Theodora Augusta, a worshipper of Pluto, sets in motion a plan. Epidamnos, the warrior-magus, also called Avian, is tasked with reuniting his colleagues, the most fearsome band of mercenaries to ever exist. Or at least those of them that survive: there was a reason they split up. Camarina the Panther, deposed princess of Thrace; Triada, an Amazonian archer (called here the archeress); the Eagle, a scarred general: he summons them all by means of their Edessa stones. Khorsabad Three-Hands he recovers from a prison in the district of thieves. Their mission: to recover the treasure offered by the Roman emperors to the old gods as an apology for ditching them in favour of Christianity. Or at least that's what they think. This digital album is the first in a series of four (all of which are also available in a single paperback collection), and it does a good job of drawing the team

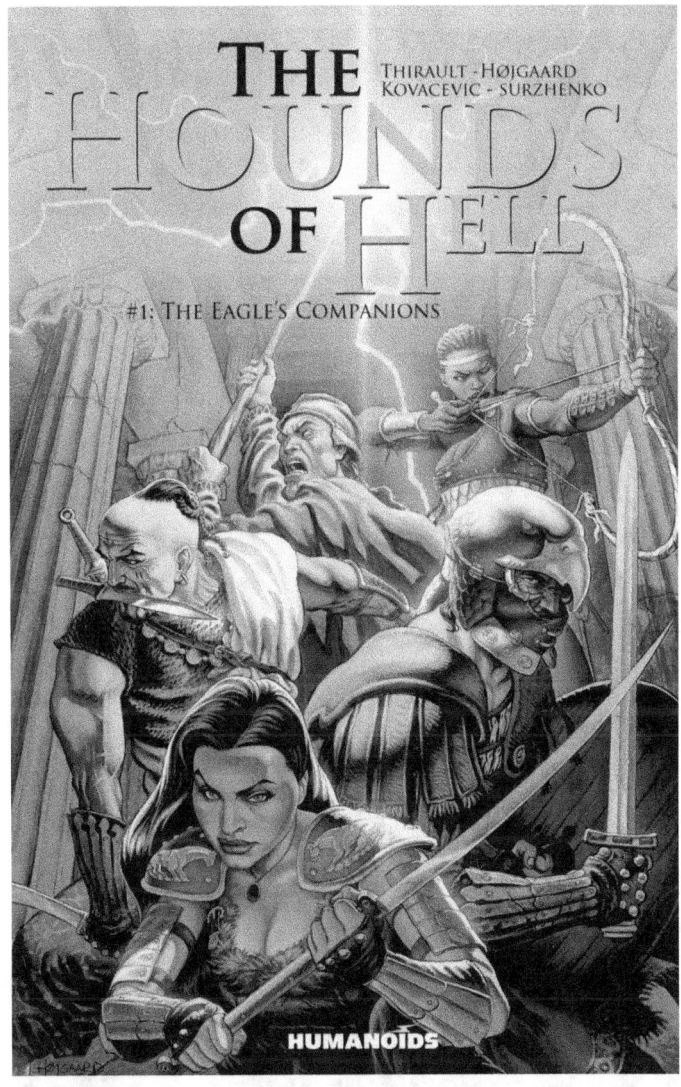

THIRAULT - HØJGAARD
KOVACEVIC - SURZHENKO

THE HOUNDS OF HELL

#1: THE EAGLE'S COMPANIONS

HUMANOÏDS

together, showing us what is special about each of them, and getting them started on their adventures, as well as dipping back into their histories. There's some unpleasant sexual violence, but otherwise it's an exciting, intriguing adventure that is impeccably drawn and coloured. *Stephen Theaker* ★★★☆☆

Locke & Key, Vol. 6: Alpha & Omega, by Joe Hill and Gabriel Rodriguez (IDW Publishing)

Since the Locke family moved to the town of Lovecraft, Massachusetts, and began to live in the big old Keyhouse, things have been weird, dangerous and magical. By the time this final collection begins the

children have almost got to the point where they can cope with their losses and new responsiblities, but the demon that possessed Luke Caravaggio is hiding among them, gathering keys of power and waiting for the most devastating time to strike: prom night, when the kids are planning to have an afterparty in the cave down by the ocean. Just where he wants them. Luckily Tyler, Kinsey and Bode have found friends and allies since they came to town, so they won't have to face this fight alone. Writer Joe Hill and artist Gabriel Rodriguez bring their story to a satisfying conclusion. The stakes are high, the heroes are brave, the villain is vile, and thematically it all ties up with where it began, Tyler telling the bad guy, "I wouldn't underrate the power of regret. It doesn't feel good... but it's hard to learn anything important without it." That's "Omega", and in the epilogue, "Alpha", Tyler makes some kind of peace with his own great regret. It's a good place for the story to end, though you feel there's still a lot of space in this world for new stories to be told. *Stephen Theaker* ★★★★☆

Marshals, Book 1: Darkness and Light, by Dennis-Pierre Filippi and Jean-Florian Tello (Humanoids)

Hisaya is a marshal on the planet Iriu, working in an area under the control of the air consortium. Her robot partner is wrecked during the apprehension of a former robo-trafficker, but her grandad can't supply her with a replacement this time: he's switched to making buxom humanoid pleasure bots (though they can fight when needed, and it will be needed). Instead he introduces her to Tetsu, a young mechanic with a passion for robotics who has built a nifty new defence bot – and she can have it if she will take Tetsu on as an apprentice. A five-page naked sauna scene with the pleasure bots later, and Marshal Hisaya returns to the city with her new apprentice and her new bot, just in time for a series of treacherous attacks that will leave everyone running for their lives. *Darkness and Light* is the first of four digital albums, also collected in a single hardcover book from the same publisher. It does a good job of setting up this steampunky, Final Fantasyesque world, and Marshal Hisaya is quite the badass. The nude scenes feel a bit redundant and pandering, and it isn't always easy to follow the action, but in general the art is very appealing and

characterful, a bit reminiscent of Ian Gibson's 200AD work, with the extra detail that working on an album rather than weekly pages can allow. The colours, by Studio Bad@ss, do a great job of picking out all that detail and letting the eye make sense of it all. A good start to the series. *Stephen Theaker* ★★★☆☆

The Savage Sword of Conan, Vol. 14, by Charles Dixon, Gary Kwapisz, Ernie Chan and chums (Dark Horse Books)

This reviewer has read several volumes in this series over the last year or so, and this review could pretty much apply to any of them, since *The Savage Sword of Conan the Barbarian* was a remarkably consistent magazine. Whichever collection you pick up, you'll get the same black-and-white mix of a rough but honourable barbarian, extremely attractive women (variously good and evil), mad wizards and kings, and reliably good storytelling and art – all for a bargain price. One improvement is that by the issues collected here, 141 to 150, the black caption boxes that made the earliest books rather a pest to read are long gone, and the creative team of Dixon, Kwapisz and Chan have settled in for a run of consecutive issues that tell a series of consecutive stories in Conan's life. As ever, each individual story, whether it is teaming up with Red Sonja on a quest for a hidden idol, defending a fort from a Pictish attack, or a struggle in Brythunia to prevent the rising of Oranah, the Stag God, who drives farmers mad with murderlust, has the length and heft of a French album, but this time they also add up to more, a grand saga that takes Conan from a gladiator to a general and beyond. One story, "Blind Vengeance", features a firm but unfair tyrant who intimidates villagers into handing over their goods, and carves a W into the foreheads of corpses – an inspiration for

Negan on *The Walking Dead*, perhaps? The speech
balloon placement is a bit careless, with the correct
reading order often counterintuitive and confusing,
but the artwork is nearly always top notch, and
unusually for a Comixology edition double page
spreads are presented as two separate pages, which

makes it much easier to read on a tablet.
Recommended to anyone who liked any of the other
volumes. *Stephen Theaker* ★★★★☆

Star Trek, Vol. 1, by Mike Johnson, Stephen Molnar and Joe Phillips (IDW Publishing)

The ongoing Star Trek comic follows the adventures of
the Chris Pine version of Captain James Kirk and his
crew, as shown in *Star Trek* XI, XII and XIII. This first
volume collects issues one to four, set soon after the
eleventh film, with Kirk in charge of the *USS
Enterprise* a good deal sooner than in the previous
continuity, and the five year mission off to an early

start. Oddly, though, they still run into many of the same situations, since the two stories here are adapted from the television episodes "Where No Man Has Gone Before", in which crewman Gary Seven acquires the powers of a god after the *Enterprise* tries to cross the galaxy's edge , and "The Galileo Seven", in which a shuttlecraft crew led by an as-yet untrusted Spock is lost and stranded on a dangerous world with aggressive locals. James Blish's prose adaptations tended to improve on the original programme, so maybe these comics could do the same? Sadly not. Adapting forty-minute episodes to forty-page comics doesn't leave room for a lot of detail, and although the stories are subtly changed by taking place in the new continuity they feel sketchy and underfed. The artwork is good, the likenesses pretty decent, it's just that the project itself feels a bit pointless. Perhaps it's aimed at fans of the new films who haven't watched the original show? Either way, it's good to see that subsequent volumes add new, original stories to the mix. *Stephen Theaker* ★★☆☆☆

Star Trek: Gold Key Archives, Vol. 1, by Dick Wood, Alberto Giolitti and Nevio Zeccara (IDW Publishing)

Back when the William Shatner version of Captain James Kirk first commanded the *USS Enterprise*, Gold Key published these cheesy but energetic stories about him and his crew; even in those early days for the franchise, half-Vulcan first officer Spock must have been the clear breakout character, since he appears more prominently than the captain on four of the six covers. Tony Isabella explains in the introduction that none of the creators involved in this series saw any episodes before starting work, which may explain why Scotty is in these issues an awkward blonde, and why in "The Planet of No Return" an encounter with a plant civilisation ends with the planet being scoured of all life, on Spock's urgent recommendation. In "The Devil's Isle of Space" the crew nonchalantly leaves convicts to be killed in an explosion, simply because it is "the *way* of their society". These are big-scale stories where anything goes. In "Invasion of the City Builders", a planet's land has been almost completely covered by

cities, thanks to automation gone too far, and "The Peril of Planet Quick Change" features missiles being fired into the planet's core. In "The Ghost Planet" the ship drags the rings away from a planet, and in "When Planets Collide" the ship must somehow stop two worlds from crashing into each other, an impact which would pitch many of the planets of the Alpho galaxy "out of orbit... to burn in space!" Galaxies seem to be quite small here, and the ship seems to visit a new one every issue! Time is measured in lunar hours and galaxy seconds, everyone in the universe speaks Space Esperanto, and Kirk calls aliens "space scum". So the stories are goofy, but that only makes them more enjoyable. It does capture that sense from the original series that the universe was an incredibly dangerous place where even heroes like Kirk and Spock would only survive if luck was on their side. The newly recoloured art looks great, and the simple six-panel grid layout makes for very easy reading. *Stephen Theaker* ★★★☆☆

The Zombies That Ate the World, Vol. 1: An Unbearable Smell! by Jerry Frissen and Guy Davis (Humanoids)

This digital album tells four of the "everyday occurrences that happen in the twilight of Los Angeles", to quote the line that ends them all. It is 2064 and the dead have been coming back to life. They aren't violent, at least no more than they were when they were alive, and so the government has decreed that the living and the dead must live peacefully together. That's going pretty well until Otto Maddox, a filthy rich man with extremely expensive hobbies, has an actor disinterred, Franza Kozik. When alive, she starred in such films as *Queen of the Zombies* and *Flesh Feast*, and once out of her coffin she picks up where she left off, eating brains, but for real this time, and that inspires other zombies to try it too. The other stories here include a historian of the twentieth century who wants his reanimated father-in-law peacefully disposed of, and a Nazi type who wants the brain of a particular zombie rewired to restore its intelligence. All four stories feature, to a greater or

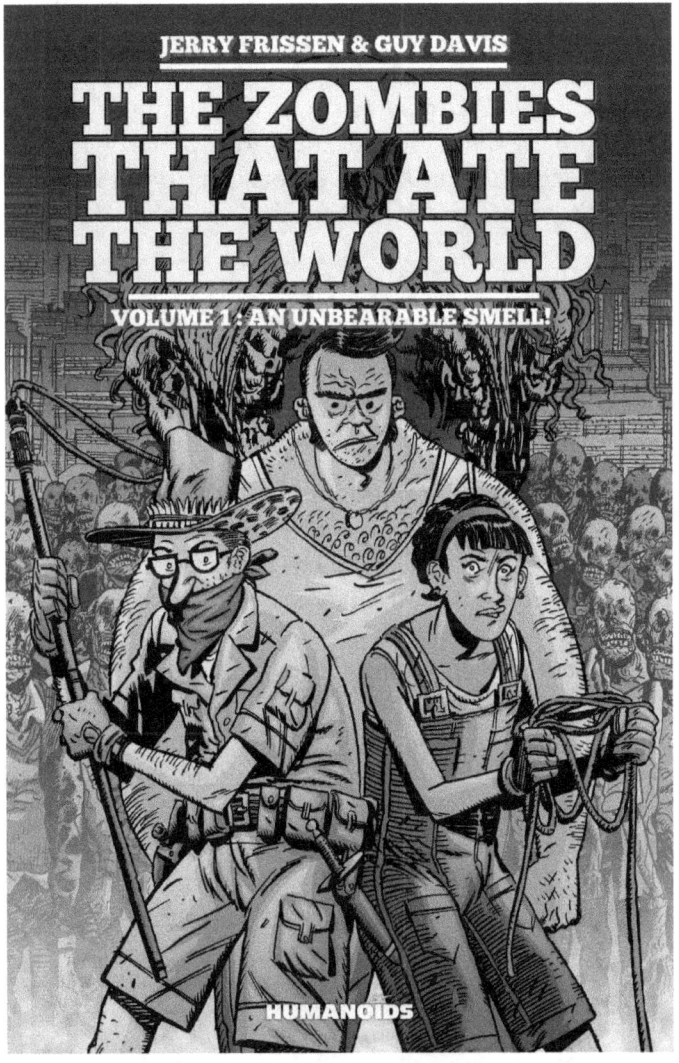

lesser extent, Karl Heard, who with his sister Maggie and their hulking associate The Belgian, makes a barely legal living as a zombie catcher. Elsewhere, Christians are executing thousands of people in the Holy Land in hopes of persuading Jesus to return, and a scientist has reanimated a dinosaur. This is an odd book, with a humorous tone that sits a bit uneasily with the tawdry and horrible stories it is telling, but it is worth reading, especially for the art of Guy Davis, who readers might know from *Sandman Mystery Theatre* or *The Marquis*. His style of drawing is exceptionally well-suited to the portrayal of the rotting undead, not to mention the other sleazy types in the book. *Stephen Theaker* ★★★☆☆

Films

Captain America: Civil War, by Christopher Markus and Stephen McFeely (Marvel Entertainment et al.)

More heroes... more fights... more fun!

Every time a new Avengers offering comes out, the filmmakers have to raise the bar for the easily distracted contemporary moviegoer ever poised to grow weary of today's superhero blitz. The fast-paced and effects-packed *Captain America: Civil War*, directed by Anthony and Joe Russo, manages to keep the Avengers juggernaut barrelling forward.

It's the typical talk fight talk fight superhero formula. Our favorite egomaniac Tony Stark/Iron Man offers the most entertaining repartee, while the spirited battle action ranges from Natasha Romanoff's/Black Widow's acrobatics to the monumental airport battle that earns the film its name. These films just keep getting bigger, faster, and more intense.

Taking Sides

The action starts in Lagos, where Wanda Maximoff/Scarlet Witch uses her psychokinetic powers to lift an active bomb out of harm's way. However, it detonates before it gets to the top of a building and there are civilian casualties. This opens up an investigation into the many fatalities left in the wake of those thrilling Avengers battles. It also leads to the split that propels the film: in an uncharacteristic move, a guilt-ridden Stark encourages the Avengers to sign a UN-sanctioned accord that limits their previously unchecked authority. Conversely, Steve Rogers/Captain America, the hitherto obedient soldier, refuses to sign because he trusts in his own (and the Avengers') superior morality and decision-making abilities.

Rogers has something else to worry about: protecting his mentally unstable WWII friend Bucky Barnes (aka Winter Soldier), the tenacious assassin of the last Captain America film. Bucky is a suspected terrorist and former Hydra pawn wanted by the same authorities that seek to limit the Avengers' powers.

So Iron Man and Captain America each build a six-person army that leads to the airport conflagration. But none of this is all that original, is it? After all, we've seen this kind of freaks versus commoners and superhero infighting since *X-Men* (2000). However, what follows shows how *Captain America: Civil War* takes things in a new direction.

Battle Aftermath Exploration

For a couple decades, we've watched mutants, shapeshifting robots, and superheroes tear apart a variety of settings in their epic battles. However, as we chomped our popcorn, did we ever think about the toll that all this destruction takes on bystanders? In a brilliant "What if..." consideration, the makers of

Captain America: Civil War pose this challenge to the heroes and in so doing, explore the pros and cons of utilitarianism.

It's About the Conflict Within
Captain America: Civil War does have a minor villain (with a strong motivation). However, unlike *X-Men*, this film focuses on the conflict between our beloved heroes, and it's a strategy that makes the logical viewer

uncomfortable. It's impossible to choose a side; they all think they're doing the right thing. Every time Iron Man blasted away at Captain America, I cringed. Every time Captain America hammered away at Iron Man, I cringed.

Stark: "I'm trying to keep you from tearing the Avengers apart." Rogers: "You did that when you signed." Yikes!

New Characters

Note that the movie poster for *Captain America: Civil War* shows a faceoff between two sets of five characters, yet I said that each side has six. That's because two characters new to the Avengers universe make an appearance. The filmmakers make it seem like these two characters are a secret, knowing full well that they will build buzz for the film. That's a brilliant marketing strategy.

Scott Lang/Ant-Man enters the scene like a little boy, thrilled just to be asked to be part of Captain America's team. Look for the film's funniest quote when Ant-Man takes off his helmet after one skirmish.

A barely post-pubescent Peter Parker/Spider-Man takes a bit more convincing to join Stark's side. Parker has homework, after all. In the film's most entertaining talk scene, Stark drops in on the apartment of Parker and a refurbished (and much more attractive) Aunt May (Marisa Tomei). Tom Holland's Parker is an energetic and chatty "little guy" who adds some youthful zeal to the Avengers, like when he refers to "that really old movie *Empire Strikes Back*".

"That Cat Guy"

Do we really need the hero that one audience member referred to as "that cat guy?" Or was T'Challa/Black Panther, with his cat ears and metal claws, just thrown into the fray because the filmmakers couldn't afford

The Hulk or Thor and they needed a sixth man to round out Stark's team? And how come this Black Panther, not genetically modified like Rogers or Bucky, can run fast enough to keep up with cars?

However, in Black Panther's defense, he does bring a kind of peripheral motivation to the conflict: his singular goal is to kill Bucky.

This is a minor irritant in an otherwise absorbing film that offers everything from the clashing humour of Captain America driving a Volkswagen Beetle to the expression of virtue through action (or inaction). I am tempted to conclude this review with some witticism regarding the brilliance of this film. Alas, instead I resort to the comment of a boy: "those fights were awesome!" *Douglas J. Ogurek* ★★★★★

The Huntsman: Winter's War, by Evan Spiliotopoulos and Craig Mazin (Roth Films/Universal Pictures)

Angry, beautiful women with ostentatious wardrobes cast spells, voyeuristic tiny creatures hide in trees, and much more.

The Huntsman: Winter's War, directed by Cedric Nicolas-Troyan, gave me what I expected, and I'm good with that. This sequel to *Snow White and the Huntsman* (2012) isn't mind-blowing. It doesn't present anything staggeringly original, nor will it change your life with some profound message, but it will allow you to escape into a fantasy world rich in costumes, effects, atmosphere, and justice.

When jilted by her forbidden lover, Freya (Emily Blunt) discovers her ability to conjure and manipulate ice, then retreats to "the north" to build an empire. A reclusive ice queen? Hmm... that sounds a lot like Elsa from *Frozen* (2013). However, Freya's blood runs much colder: her manipulative sister Ravenna (Charlize

Theron), now trapped in Snow White's famous mirror, is the spellbinding supervillain who fumed and enchanted her way through the first film.

Queen Freya seizes children to raise as an army of fierce warriors (the huntsmen), which she uses to expand her kingdom. She imposes only one rule on her adult "children": no love allowed! But huntsmen standouts Eric (Chris Hemsworth) and Sara (Jessica Chastain) aren't having it. So Freya uses her sorcery to separate the lovers.

Years later, Eric and Sara reunite, albeit discordantly, on a quest to retrieve the now lost magic mirror before Freya gets it and catastrophe ensues. They are joined by four dwarves, highlighted by Nion (Nick Frost) and the feisty widow Mrs Bromwyn (Sheridan Smith).

Though *Winter's War* advertisements exhibit the villainous sisters in all their regal splendour, the film offers a more traditional hero. Eric faces the dual challenge of finding that mirror (i.e. saving the world) and convincing Sara of his constancy. Our hero smiles, chuckles, and tosses around his machismo in typical Hemsworth fashion.

It's Not Plot
And what will this band of likely and unlikely heroes do when it gets the mirror? Does it really matter? The mirror is really just a device holding things together. The strength of *Winter's War* lies not in plot or concept, but in the special effects that, like the gold flakes around Ravenna's eyes, sparkle throughout the film to create an atmosphere.

Besides the sisters' conjurations – more on this later – the special effects engineers rise to the challenge with a collection of CGI creatures that populate this fairy tale world: too-small-to-see sprites that leave light trails in their wake, bright red squirrels, swarms of butterflies hitching a ride on a hedgehog, bling-wearing goblins that look and move like apes but have ram-like horns, and turtles and snakes with skin made out of grass. Then there are the voyeuristic, pint-size slender creatures that hide in vegetation and silently watch the adventurers. Creepy. Cool.

Winter's War also offers several rousing fight scenes, especially the quarrels at the palace entry and tavern. The tension builds, the outnumbered heroes remain remarkably calm, the enemies assemble, and then the powerful Eric and acrobatic Sara deliver a beat down... or get beat up. The lack of music during these scenes adds to the intensity by emphasizing the thumping, crashing, and other skirmish sounds.

Sisters Sorcerous and Sexy
Someone once said, "There's nothing quite like angry, beautiful women in glittering regalia working magic." Actually, I don't think anyone said that, but there is some truth to it.

The film treats Freya and Ravenna with the reverence that royalty commands. For instance, the grandeur of the sisters' costumes gets elevated by audio embellishments such as the chain-like slinking of Queen Freya's train as she promenades toward her captives, or the metal finger claws that Ravenna taps and scrapes on various surfaces.

Freya is the subdued, though still highly dangerous version of her older sister. Her finery glistens like frost and offers a contrast of colourless austerity and glittering flamboyance much like the character. Example: she might tear up while she casts a spell that ruins a person's life.

But don't expect any tears from Ravenna, unless they're tears of rage. The only criticism of Theron's ruthless sorceress is that she isn't on the screen more. Indulge in Theron's mastery of her craft as she greets

Eric after a long absence, slathers a supervillain laugh over her adversaries, and seduces her chess partner.

During the climax, the sisters use Freya's royal hall to put on a rock concert of sorcery, their instruments being ice (Freya) and tar-like tentacles (Ravenna) that aim to impale.

When life's pressures mount, mindless fantasy films like this one offer a much-needed respite. I've seen

characters using magic powers to freeze stuff. I've seen goblins and dwarves. I've seen super clear distinctions between good and evil. And I don't mind seeing it all again: that stuff's therapeutic. *Douglas J. Ogurek*
★★★★☆

Independence Day: Resurgence, by Nicolas Wright et al. (Stereo D et al.)

Like the first one... just much worse.

Although President (Bill Pullman) Whitmore's rousing speech in *Independence Day* (1996) is clichéd and overly dramatic, people can't help but love it. It makes them feel something.

The makers of *Independence Day: Resurgence* had to make sure that Whitmore gave another speech. This time, the dishevelled and over-medicated has-been attempts to do so in an airport hangar. Music plays. People gather. At the end, the smirk of David Levinson (Jeff Goldblum) seems to say, "Yeah, nowhere near as good as your first one." Such is the sentiment that summarises this film.

Independence Day, though far from a masterpiece, gained many fans. It showed nations uniting for a common cause. It revealed Will Smith's emerging talent. It gave us the zaniness of Dr Brackish Okun, as well as Whitmore's "Nuke 'em. Let's nuke the bastards." It even started this whole monument destruction thing.

Roland Emmerich returns to direct a Smith-less (and witless) sequel that tries too hard to be like its predecessor. Major characters make sacrifices that fizzle, excessive pilot whooping gets annoying, skies filled with aircraft and lasers grow tedious, and attempts to stir emotion fall flat. In fact, the big idea of this film (i.e. aliens attack Earth, humans fight back) duplicates that of the first. Why even make this sequel?

The film takes place in a rainbows and butterflies (e.g. no terrorism, peace between nations) alternate present twenty years after the alien attack. You will hear that twenty years have elapsed again and again and again: two decades ago, 1996, twenty years ago, 7,000 days. Enough already!

It's easy to see very early in the film why critics

ripped this one apart: shallow characters, sub-par to abysmal acting, and expository dialogue.

Since this is an event movie, it presents no clearly defined protagonist. Instead, we are left with a stumbling cast of new characters, including dull pilots, a not-so-funny comic relief, Whitmore's forgettable daughter, a sabre-wielding, scowling African warlord whose attempts at drama are laughable, and a psychiatrist who specializes in alien mind control. Then there are all the returning characters stuffed into the film.

One of the cast's two saving graces is Jeff Goldblum, whose quirky walk and idiosyncratic speaking style always entertain. I'm paraphrasing here: "There's a queen in there... a very... big... queen." Goldblum's professorial demeanour makes the film's juvenile objective (i.e. blow up the bad guy) seem like a brilliant scientific deduction.

The raggedy Dr Brackish Okun (Brent Spiner), who springs up after a 20-year coma with his mind teeming with alien formulae, is another favorite. However, even his maniacal approach doesn't have the same oomph as it did in *Independence Day*. Okun does manage to pull off the film's one scene that transfers emotion to the viewer.

Where are the filmmakers trying to go with this movie? Are they trying to be silly-serious in the vein of *Ghost Rider* (2007)? They don't succeed. Are they trying to tap into viewers' emotions? They're way off base: the film has too many palm-slapped-against-forehead failed attempts to wring out emotion. Ultimately, *Independence Day: Resurgence*, hovering somewhere between sci-fi drama and comedy, doesn't know what it wants to be.

When I saw *Independence Day* twenty years ago, my fellow theatregoers responded with an intensity of clapping that I've never seen matched. After

Independence Day: Resurgence, the theatre, though full, was silent. Do yourself a favour: just watch the original again. *Douglas J. Ogurek* ★★★☆☆

Innerspace, by Jeffrey Boam and Chip Proser (Warner Bros. et al.)

Dir. Joe Dante. 1 July 1987 (Amblin Entertainment). Genre: SF Comedy. Ratings: 81% (Rotten Tomatoes) 6.7 (IMDB).

Obstreperous test pilot Tuck Pendleton (Dennis Quaid) volunteers for a miniaturisation experiment that should see him and his ship injected into the bloodstream of a laboratory rabbit. Instead, thanks to some industrial espionage gone badly wrong, he finds himself inside hypochondriac no-hoper Jack Putter (Martin Short). Aided by Pendleton's ex-girlfriend, journalist Lydia Maxwell (Meg Ryan), and guided from within by Pendleton himself, Putter must overcome his inhibitions, thwart the villains and recover the microchip necessary to extract the ship before Pendleton's oxygen runs out.

Steven Spielberg virtually owned the 1980s, and as executive producer added a tenuous sort of clout to several films in which he had no real involvement. *Innerspace* was one such production, its title invariably being sandwiched between the words "Steven Spielberg presents" and "a Joe Dante film" (this combination having in 1984 brought *Gremlins* to the cinema and thus being judged likely to wow prospective viewers into the right frame of mind). But *Innerspace* was no *Close Encounters of the Third Kind* (1977), *Raiders of the Lost Ark* (1981) or *E.T. the Extra-Terrestrial* (1982). It was, rather, an unabashedly silly reworking of *Fantastic Voyage* (1966), the cold war SF-adventure that provided Raquel Welch with her breakout role and by way of its novelisation added

considerably to Isaac Asimov's renown. Although
Asimov did his best to make the written version more
palatable, *Fantastic Voyage* sacrificed science for
adventure and presented audiences with several
indigestible, illogical dollops of plot tripe. *Innerspace*
proved equally loose in favouring comedy over
accuracy, and despite winning an Academy Award for
Best Visual Effects – the internal landscape of Putter's
body is impressively realised – clearly made no effort
at all to keep the scale of miniaturisation either
believable or consistent. (Hence, in accordance with
industry standards for advertising, the tagline: "An
Adventure of Incredible Proportions".) But this should
come as no surprise; after all, the entire movie is a
paean to the culture, filmmaking and associated
extravagances in kitsch of the 1980s, where over-quirky
meets over-the-top and the minor characters are
served up as a layered profiterole cake of coiffured
oddballs. Fans of *The Blues Brothers* (1980) may take
some heart in seeing Henry Gibson (Nazi leader) cast
here as Putter's affably anxious boss, but whereas there
was a dreamlike quality in the Illinois Nazis having
driven past the back-flipping Bluesmobile and off an
unfinished highway ramp, thence to fall over a
hundred storeys and land directly in front of that same
speeding Bluesmobile, the incongruity throughout
Innerspace tends more towards that of an overt, in-
your-face surrealistic slap. Recently contemporaneous
comedies such as *Ferris Bueller's Day Off* (1986) and
Running Scared (1986) had shown what could be
achieved by injecting a measure of absurdity into real
character types, but *Innerspace* writers Jeffrey Boam
and Chip Proser clearly missed this point and instead
merely jabbed themselves, their butterfingers ensuring
that the inherent craziness of the film becomes
blurred, rather than put into sharp focus, by an
extraneous excess of background weirdness. This may

have been less evident to moviegoers at the time –
there still being, needless to say, Martin Short jangling
prominently in the foreground – but it is jarring in
retrospect, and becoming more and more so as the
eighties continue to recede, the perky novelty of the
decade fading away amidst a Cyndi Lauper-load of

bangles, leg warmers and erupting hairstyles into the nostalgic embarrassment of history.

By 1987 Martin Short already was familiar to television audiences as a performer on seasons 4–5 (1982–1983) of Canadian sketch comedy programme *SCTV* and season 10 (1984–1985) of America's *Saturday Night Live*. His big screen breakthrough had come in 1986 alongside Steve Martin and Chevy Chase in *¡Three Amigos!* while an effortless penchant for physical humour and a seemingly endless supply of woebegone expressions would later see him teamed up with Nick Nolte in *Three Fugitives* (1989) and then Danny Glover in *Pure Luck* (1991), the spirit of the times being to cast Short several times over as the hapless victim of some great cosmic irony. *Innerspace*, however, was very much his film and his alone, and all things told he succeeds quite splendiferously in carrying it along. The persona of Jack Putter has been scripted with a heavy hand, established only in broad caricature and then prodded to walk jerky steps along the plank and dive off into an ungainly character arc, while the plot map bears evidence of that same hand carefully marking out big Xs in crayon. Dennis Quaid's Tuck Pendleton is not merely a ne'er-do-well, roguish stereotype, but in fact a shameless attempt at reprising (in all but name) Harrison Ford's Han Solo (in fact, the Pendleton-Putter-Maxwell love triangle is so manifestly the same as that of Solo-Skywalker-Leia that one wonders if even today the writers are washing off stains from the carbon paper). The movie is overly manipulative in its music (Jerry Goldsmith), underwhelming in its attempts to build tension, and then again over-reliant for its impact on peak moments rather than sustained, coherent storytelling. But what moments they are: pratfalls and injuries à la Short; madcap stunts sans modern effects but heavy on flailing, panicking, Chaplinesque Short; facial transmogrifications that if played out in the political arena would have seen a Martin Short puppet battling to exorcise itself on British satire show *Spitting Image*; and, of course, the Jack Putter dance – that iconic, joyous, elastically uninhibited flailing about and letting loose of the inner hallelujah, Short's comedic chutzpah burning as red-hot-poker-bright behind retinas today as it did back in 1987, and indeed having gained some extra kudos along the way through dint of blueprinting a few of Mike Myers' moves in *Austin Powers: International Man of Mystery* (1997). This, in short (ha!), is Martin Short in his finest hour (and fifty-five minutes), and his performance is enough to make something eighties-memorable out of what otherwise would have been merely an over-long piece of second-rate children's television.

Prior to *Innerspace*, Dennis Quaid featured in paranormal thriller *Dreamscape* (1984) and SF drama *Enemy Mine* (1985). Kevin McCarthy (head villain) had starred in SF classic *Invasion of the Body Snatchers* (1956). Vernon Wells (psychotic henchman) played in the post-apocalyptic *Mad Max 2* (1981), while Wendy Schaal (disinterested second love interest) survived an *Alien*-spawned turkey, *Creature* (1985). Robert Picardo (ostentatious latin cowboy) had a minor role in Ridley Scott's dark fairy-tale *Legend* (1985), as did William Schallert (confounded scientist) in SF thriller *Colossus: the Forbin Project* (1970). Even William Bean (Lydia's editor) had warbled his epiglottis in the waters of fantasy, voicing Bilbo Baggins in an animated version of *The Hobbit* (1977). Nor were writers Jeffrey Boam and Chip Proser entirely without spec-fic experience, the former having adapted Stephen King's *The Dead Zone* (1983) and the latter having co-scripted *Iceman* (1984). Cinematographer Andrew Laszlo had worked on horror movie *Poltergeist II: The Other Side* (1986), as had composer Jerry Goldsmith, who also scored dystopian classic *Logan's Run* (1976) and SF horror masterpiece *Alien* (1979), among many others. But, of course, none of that made a scrap of difference to *Innerspace*, which remained steadfastly a comedy, its science fiction elements having little *raison d'être* beyond providing an idiosyncratic vehicle by which to convey Martin Short's virtuoso performance to the silver screen. Yes, the bunny rabbit schematic is a nice touch, but when the history books are written *Innerspace* might just warp blithely past the SF chroniclers and instead stooge its way into the tome dealing with humour, banging heads with the silent comics and going, "Nyuk-nyuk-nyuk!" as the first film ever to deliver a poke in the eye from the inside. *Jacob Edwards*

The Legend of Tarzan, by Adam Cozad and Craig Brewer (Dark Horse Entertainment et al.)

New take on classic story swings engagingly between action, setting, and character.

Whether you've confronted Tarzan in a comic book, a Disney cartoon, or Edgar Rice Burroughs's novels, chances are you don't envision the iconic jungle-dwelling adventurer as a tea drinker.

However, sipping tea among British diplomats is exactly what the now civilized hero (Alexander Skarsgård) is doing when we meet him in *The Legend of Tarzan*, directed by David Yates. The man raised by apes wants his colleagues to address him not as Tarzan, but rather as John Clayton III, Lord of Greystoke. But that's not what we viewers want!

So comes the call to adventure. Tarzan sets out to his motherland, the African Congo, with wife Jane (Margot Robbie) and gun slinger George Washington Williams (Samuel L. Jackson) to save his countrymen from slavery at the hand of Belgium's King Leopold, who's exploiting the land for his own gain.

Unbeknownst to Tarzan, Leopold's chief envoy Leon Rom, masterfully played by Christoph Waltz, has promised Chief Mbonga (Djimon Hounsou) that he will deliver Tarzan in exchange for the coveted diamonds of Opar. To up his odds, Rom captures Jane to lure Tarzan. Thus begins our ultra-ripped hero's swinging, hollering, brawling quest punctuated by flashbacks to his jungle upbringing.

If you're a huge fan of *Mad Max: Fury Road* (2015) type nonstop zany action, then *The Legend of Tarzan* probably isn't for you. However, if you approach this film with the same patience and reverence with which Tarzan approaches a cup of tea (or a lion), then you can walk away more than satisfied. Tarzan is, at its core, a damsel in distress story that shows the lengths to which an alpha male will go to save his mate (and his friends). It offers a sufficient dose of action including jungle acrobatics, battling troops and tribes, and attempting to escape the jungle's deadliest creatures. Tarzan even takes on his gorilla brother in an attempt to regain his standing within the band. Sure, the film is rife with Hollywoodisms – watch for a gorilla waving on a herd of stampeding wildebeests – but isn't that part of the Tarzan charm?

The film's true strength lies more in its devotion to setting. *The Legend of Tarzan* is, above all, a milieu story about exploring a world much different to ours. This Tarzan isn't an eccentric or complicated guy, but then again, he never was. Tarzan and the jungle are indelibly linked, and this film shows that relationship in his interactions with the natives and with the majestic creatures that today hover on the brink of extinction.

Another strength is the always entertaining Christoph Waltz, who tones down his typical verbosity with a more reserved Leon Rom. Though his panama suit and hat and the rosary he constantly clutches suggest a pious individual, Rom is anything but. He uses that rosary, made of super strong material, to strangle those who stand in his way.

Despite the outdoors focus, the film's most entertaining scene occurs in the dining quarters of Rom's boat, where we get to see Waltz in his element...

table talk, that is (see *Inglorious Basterds* (2009) or *Django Unchained* (2012) for shining examples). Here Rom attempts to host a cordial meal with his captive Jane. While his outward civility masks his true intent of testing Jane, Rom's facial expressions, smiles, diction, and attentiveness to his guest serve up a delicacy at this cinematic feast. He even reaches over the table to reposition one of Jane's utensils on her plate after she leaves.

Comedy relief sidekicks have the potential to be annoying, but Samuel L. Jackson makes it work as George Washington Williams. Williams spends most of this film trying to keep up with the hero, expressing shock, and commenting on Tarzan's abilities. It's as if he's nudging the viewer and saying, "Can you believe this guy?"

Tarzan swings through the jungle. He cuddles with lions. He takes on gorillas and small armies. That *is* hard to believe. It's also the stuff of legends. *Douglas J. Ogurek* ★★★★★

X-Men: Apocalypse, by Simon Kinberg (Twentieth Century Fox Film Corporation et al.)

The events of *X-Men: Days of Future Past* have changed the timeline, and everyone now knows about mutants. Mystique is a hero to her kind, a civil rights leader who runs an underground railroad to help the less fortunate among them, such as Nightcrawler, forced to fight in a cage match against a very angry Angel. Back in Westchester, Professor Xavier has got his school for the gifted up and running, and when Magneto resurfaces, recruited by Apocalypse during a vulnerable moment, Mystique goes to Xavier for help. Cyclops and Jean Gray are already there, learning to control their powers, and Quicksilver is on his way – he also wants to find Magneto, albeit for different reasons. It'll take the lot of them to cope with Apocalypse, an ancient body-swapping, power-collecting mutant who has just escaped from his underground prison of thousands of years. He's a tough cookie and he can be very persuasive. It is time for the X-Men to go into action for the very first time all over again, and that is part of this film's joy, to see a team very close to that of the Claremont/Byrne years of the comic in action: Cyclops, Jean Gray, Beast, Nightcrawler, Professor Xavier and even Storm, though she's on the wrong side for much of the film, Apocalypse having found her in this timeline in Cairo before Xavier got around to it. It's great to see them together, and that contributes to this feeling like the most X-Meny of the X-Men films yet. *X2: X-Men United* may have been a better film overall, but it felt like a science fiction film based on the idea of the X-Men whereas this feels like the X-Men. The melodrama, the humour, the flips from one side to the other, the bravery and tragedy: it's all here. Once again Quicksilver comes close to stealing the film. Psylocke is introduced, but her complicated backstory is perhaps wisely left to one side, so there's no sign of her brother Captain Britain, sadly. Another much-loved character makes an extremely violent five-minute cameo that may leave parents wondering whether it was wise to bring children to the film, as well as wondering how it ties up with the conclusion of the previous film – but continuity has never really been a concern of these films. See how badly the end of *The Wolverine* lines up with the beginning of *Days of Future Past*, or the constant recasting of any character not played by Hugh Jackman. By this ninth film in the series, including all spin-offs, that discontinuity must be taken as read. Let's just assume there are changes to the timeline going on constantly in this movie universe, not just those we see on screen. It's not

perfect by any means – the tears over the lost cast of *X-Men: First Class* seem insincere given the film-maker's decision to give them the boot. The post-credits scene is a colossal letdown, leaving the cinema audience audibly deflated (ironic for a film that credits its inflatable audience wranglers). But overall it was probably my favourite X-Men film yet. It rounds off this prequel trilogy nicely, James McAvoy being especially fantastic as Professor Xavier, while setting things up very well for what could be a new set of films featuring the classic line-up in their youth. I'm looking forward to the next film much more than I was looking forward to this one. *Stephen Theaker*
★★★☆☆

X-Men: Apocalypse (take two), by Simon Kinberg (Twentieth Century Fox Film Corporation et al.)

Prepare for what might be the most entertaining action scene that you've ever experienced.

I thought that these X-Men movies would start running out of gas, but they haven't... and I don't want them to. *X-Men: Apocalypse*, the latest installment in the longstanding series, keeps it moving full speed ahead. Director Bryan Singer serves up his fifth X-Men work with all the ingredients of a great action/adventure: humour, loss, vengeance, spectacular visuals, great music (ranging from Beethoven to Metallica), extreme character change, and of course, violence. Plus we find out how Ororo Munroe/Storm got white hair and how Professor Charles Xavier lost his hair. Bam!

And yes, the film rather blatantly jumps on the apocalypse bandwagon, but so what? If people like the prospect of a destroyed Earth, then give them that.

In an alternate 1983, En Sabah Nur/Apocalypse, the world's first mutant, awakens in Cairo after a 5,500-

year nap. The supervillain recruits four susceptible mutants (just like four horsemen, eh?), then sets out to conquer the world. A larger group of mutants, headed by younger versions of the ever peaceful Charles Xavier and the pre-antihuman Raven/Mystique, wants to stop them.

There are many fun tidbits sprinkled throughout the film. Following are a few examples:

- Storm hurls lightning while screaming like a tennis player.
- Kurt Wagner/Nightstalker wears Michael Jackson's famous red leather jacket.
- Jean Grey reveals her extreme power (and a little of her mental instability).
- After two characters say that Mystique's heroics changed their lives, Peter Maximoff/Quicksilver says, "Mine too. I mean, I still live in my mom's basement, but pfft. Everything else is, uh… well, it's pretty much the same. I'm a total loser."

Acting ranges from satisfactory to great. It reaches its peak with Michael Fassbender's Erik Lehnsherr/Magneto. Since the havoc he wreaked in *X-Men: Days of Future Past* (2014), Erik has retreated to a Polish village, started a family, and become a dependable blue collar worker. However, tragedy must strike to put this metal manipulator on the path to villainy. It's difficult for an actor to convincingly convey grief in a superhero film, but Fassbender pulls it off.

Oscar Isaac delivers an enjoyably over-the-top bad guy in En Sabah Nur/Apocalypse (aren't the most ridiculous villains often the most entertaining?). He kills people by merging them into walls or the ground. His vocals shift between a whisper and a multi-voice roar: "Everything they've built will fall! And from the ashes of their world, we'll build a better one!"

A Speedster and a Maniac
Even for those who think it's time to put a big X over this franchise, it would be downright inhuman not to enjoy the two best scenes, which are really only peripherally connected to the plot. The first begins when the film speed slows, the camera focuses on a bee, and synthesizers kick off the Eurythmics' eighties classic "Sweet Dreams". Then the super-fast Peter Maximoff/Quicksilver (Evan Peters) steps into the

scene. Prepare to laugh out loud and be awed as Peter attempts to save other mutants from an exploding building. Because it's from his perspective, everything around him appears in slow motion. Watch him backtrack to save an airbound fish, then grimace as two youngsters lean in for a sloppy kiss. If you saw Peter's talents displayed in a similar scene in *X-Men: Days of Future Past*, then you're in for a treat: this one takes it to the next level. At the film's end, the woman next to me said, "That was the best action scene I've ever seen."

The second standout scene could be interpreted as a cameo trick to boost box office sales, but doesn't everyone love a good trick? In it, a shirtless Wolverine goes on a rage-induced killing spree during which he uses his new adamantium claws to slice and impale his way through 40 or 50 men before running out into the snow. No talking. No magic. Just growling and slashing and killing. Raw power. As Wolverine retreats, a stunned Scott Summers/Cyclops can only say, "Hope that's the last we've seen of that guy."

In the Moment
Certainly there are things that the fussy moviegoer can pick apart. That's partly because there's so much chronological shifting in the X-Men series. So questions emerge: Shouldn't character A and character B be closer in age? Didn't character C first meet character D much later?

Moreover, the underdeveloped Raven/Mystique character didn't require an actress of Jennifer Lawrence's calibre, and the "adult" Mystique of earlier instalments was more "mystiquey".

Then there are the typical critic jabs (e.g. "tired", "unimaginative") that seem to come with any long-lasting series. Maybe they stepped out to sharpen their critical spears during the scenes with Quicksilver and Wolverine.

Here's some advice for watching this film: enjoy it in the moment. *Douglas J. Ogurek* ★★★★★

Notes

Also Received, But Not Yet Reviewed
Notes by Stephen Theaker

- Essex, Sophie (ed.), *A Galaxy of Starfish: an Anthology of Modern Surrealism* (Salo Press): already sold out, I think, so my review may end up being a little redundant!
- Flynn, S.C., *Children of the Different* (The Hive)
- Hughes, Matthew, *A Wizard's Henchman* (PS Publishing): first book of the Kaslo Chronicles, from one of my favourite writers.
- Lovegrove, James, *Age of Heroes* (Rebellion): from another of my current favourites, this looks great.
- Reynolds, Alastair, *Revenger* (Gollancz)
- Satifka, Erica L., *Stay Crazy* (Apex Publications)
- Whiston, Daniel, and chums, *Neroy Sphinx: Back in the Game* (Futurequake Press): graphic novel with a foreword from James Lovegrove.

About TQF

Copyright

ISBN (print): 978-1-910387-17-7
ISBN (epub): 978-1-910387-18-4

ISSN (print): 1747-6083
ISSN (online): 1747-6075

Website: www.theakersquarterly.blogspot.com

Email: theakersquarterlyfiction@gmail.com

Lulu Store: www.lulu.com/silveragebooks

Feedbooks: www.feedbooks.com/userbooks/tag/tqf

Submissions: Submissions are very welcome! See website for guidelines and terms.

Advertising: We welcome ad swaps with small press publishers and other creative types, and we'll run ads for relevant new projects from former contributors.

Sending material for review: We are interested in reviewing almost anything that's fantasy-related. We prefer to receive books for review in epub or mobi format. Feel free to send ebooks without querying first. We have reviewed about 14% of items received, though many of those reviewed are things we've actively requested from places like NetGalley.

Mission statement: The primary goal of *Theaker's Quarterly Fiction* is to keep going. If you're wondering why we do something a particular way, our primary goal is probably why.

Copyright and legal: All works are copyright the

respective authors, who have assumed all responsibility for any legal problems arising from publication of their material. Other material copyright Stephen Theaker and John Greenwood.

Published in Theaker's Paperback Library on 9 September 2016.

Other Publications

Theaker's Quarterly Fiction #55
Howard Watts (ed.)

Theaker's Quarterly Fiction #9–54
Stephen Theaker and John Greenwood (eds)

Theaker's Quarterly Fiction #1–8
Stephen Theaker (ed.)

Space University Trent: Hyperparasite
Walt Brunston

There Are Now a Billion Flowers
The Hatchling (forthcoming)
John Greenwood

The Mercury Annual
Pilgrims at the White Horizon
Michael Wyndham Thomas

The Conan Doyle Weirdbook
Rafe McGregor (ed.)

Professor Challenger in Space
Quiet, the Tin Can Brains Are Hunting!
The Fear Man
Howard Phillips in His Nerves Extruded
Howard Phillips and The Doom That Came to Sea Base Delta

Howard Phillips and The Day the Moon Wept Blood
Stephen Theaker

Five Forgotten Stories
John Hall

Elephant
Harsh Grewal

Elsewhere
Steven Gilligan

New Words #1–4
John Greenwood, Steven Gilligan
and Stephen Theaker (eds)

Forthcoming Attractions

Expect **Theaker's Quarterly Fiction #57** in October,
and **#58** in December. Reviews and continuing serials
aside, we are not now open to submissions until
January 2017.

Our blog is rather more active now:
www.theakersquarterly.blogspot.com

Stephen tweets every few days or so at:
www.twitter.com/Rolnikov

The zine now has its own Twitter account too:
www.twitter.com/TheakersQrtly

Our email address is:
theakersquarterlyfiction@gmail.com

www.ingramcontent.com/pod-product-compliance
Lightning Source LLC
Chambersburg PA
CBHW070605130626
46556CB00001B/277